What readers are saying about *The Necessaries*:

"The women in these 13 stories are a lucky number. Urban deftly reveals their wants and needs in such a way that readers feel compelled to keep turning the page to find out what's going to happen, where they will go, what they will say, do and, perhaps most importantly, what they will *think*. Urban draws you in to the circumstances of their lives through prose so keen and almost unbearably lovely that it feels both mysterious and familiar. She creates complex characters who embody seemingly conflicting ways of being and yet, by the story's end, you can't imagine there's any other way for them to navigate their lives."

—Christiana Langenberg, author of *Half of What I Know*

"The messy emotions of love and longing spill off the pages of *The Necessaries* in equal parts of razor wit and tender honesty. The stories unfold in beautiful language that treats the ear, tests the mind, and touches the heart."

—Tom McKay, author of *Another Life* and *West Fork*

"Taken together, the thirteen stories in *The Necessaries* rise to the level of a worldview: our longing for loving connections, which so often seem elusive, may be satisfied in unforeseen ways if we persevere and open ourselves to the unexpected. Vividly drawn characters speak their minds and reveal their desires on these pages as their journeys lead to quiet, stunning possibilities: love in all its varieties, romance without sentiment, gratitude as a kind of happiness, a buoyant grace."

—Mary Howard, author of *Discovering the Body* and *The Girl With Wings*

"Traversing the ordinary and the extraordinary (and everything in between), Misty Urban introduces us over and over again to our most human desire: to find connection with someone else. Her stories explore the tenuous threads of her characters' relationships with humor and grit, humility and abandon. When we're desperately looking for others, we are sometimes lucky enough to find ourselves. With *The Necessaries*, Urban has kindly allowed us to borrow the map."

—Sarah Gerkensmeyer, author of *What You Are Now Enjoying*

The Necessaries:
Stories

MISTY URBAN

Published in the United States by Paradisiac Publishing

ISBN: 0-692-70655-0
ISBN-13: 978-0-692-70655-8

DEDICATION

To Molly, Stacie, and Pam—

my necessaries

TABLE OF CONTENTS

ACKNOWLEDGEMENTS

"The Necessaries" first appeared in *Oklahoma Review* 5.2

"Ficus" first appeared in *District Lit*

"Tandem" was a favorite in the Bettendorf Public Library's 2016 short fiction contest and appeared in *The River Cities' Reader*

"Bay City" first appeared in partial form in the anthology *DOMESTIC* (Willow Press, 2017)

"Smoke Inhalation" first appeared in *Forword*, a publication by the Women's Center at Cornell University

"River Bottom" first appeared in *Fiction Attic*

"Happiness" first appeared in *The Cerurove 1*

"Flight" first appeared in *Grasslimb* 4.1

"Welcome to LulutheLesbian.com!" was an honorable mention in the 2015 novella contest held by Minerva Rising Press

THE NECESSARIES

Ben told me that the top floor of the Sears Tower moves anywhere from seven to thirteen inches in a good ripping wind. On the day we visited, riding the elevator up and down because going up just once seemed a waste, I read all the plaques on the observation deck. We stood looking out over the square concrete blocks veined with interstate and I thought of ants on a Lego farm. Ben said he thought of Godzilla. Eight shades of blue lapped like spools of ribbon out into the lake. On a clear day, the signage said, you can see all the way to Michigan.

I suppose a building could move that much. But secretly—I'm convinced of this—these skyscrapers don't want us to believe in them. They can only take so much. One day they'll decide to give up, let the top floors snap off and crash into the streets where the winds howl like an El train gone mad.

The day my mother tells me is a ten-incher, by my guess. Women clutch their skirts to their knees and leaves from the *Tribune* skirl against a grainy sky. I can see it in my mind, in slow-action black and white, the observation deck cracking, toppling, plummeting onto the steps of the courtyard right as I'm walking across it. I would dash under the shadow to grab for a small child and be pinned beneath the debris. Spectators would clap hands to their mouths in shock and horror. My officemates would declare a day off for grief. My mother would dab her eyes. "Lucy was always my sweet one," she'd say, though she has no other children.

"It's just the way it's built," Ben said as we stood at the summit of the Windy City, watching traffic back up on Lakeshore Drive. "The girders are designed to give against the stress." He pressed his nose against the observation window, leaving an obnoxious smear.

"There's no such thing as flexible steel," I said. I felt the building sway. In the plunging tube of the elevator I careened on my feet and Ben propped one careless shoulder against me. In the gift shop I looked sidewise at him through key chains and waited for him to turn to me, the light glinting meaningfully off his glasses, and say, you have the most beautiful teeth I have ever seen. You don't know what your teeth do to me.

"My mother's afraid of heights," I said, though I couldn't think of a single other thing she was afraid of.

1

"I'm not afraid of heights," Ben said, making another nose-smear next to the first. "I'm afraid of falling."

The day my mother tells me I fight through the winds to the Bongo Bar, our usual after-work watering hole, closed briefly for renovations. "I'm thinking Van Gogh, only not so many fields and stuff," Nan says, standing in the middle of the room and wheeling her arms like a windmill at the flares of blank white space. "Monet, without the flowers."

"Did you know Monet made over four hundred paintings of those lilies?" I tell her.

"Whatever for?"

"Because it wasn't quite what he wanted, I suppose. Can you imagine? Four hundred tries to get something right."

"I have less than four hundred tries," Nan says. "I have slightly less than one. If this place doesn't start making more money my landlord's going to kick me out and open a Laura Ashley shop."

Nicky's been with Nan from the start, and I do what I can for business. The Bongo Bar is her brainchild, born from all those afternoons spent drumming in Grant Park. Nan assures me that drumming has very therapeutic effects. She invited me to a session once, and I brought Ben. We were asked not to come back.

Nan slaps a hand to her head dramatically. A tiny black curl stuffed under her bandana springs back into form when she takes her hand away. "Monet!" she says again. "The Japanese garden all along this wall. Little girl, here." She directs one flannel-clad arm toward the spot. "Trellis, here. And the sunflowers, all along here. In neon paint, so you can see them in the dark."

"I'll bet Ben could find you a good painter," I offer. "A student at the Institute who would work for free."

Nan gives me a coy, sidewise look. In her bandana and overalls, with the tails of her flannel shirt sticking out the gaps in the sides, she looks like a bohemian Lolita. Next to her in my heeled boots and sweater jacket, I feel frumpy and far too tall. She starts stacking stools atop tables and I help.

"Where is Ben?" she wants to know.

"How should I know?" One of my chairs skids off the tabletop and hits the floor. "Why should I care?"

"Ah," Nan says. "Ben has offended."

"Ben has a date tonight. I doubt we'll see him."

"Good riddance," Nan says. "You can help me paint."

Behind us, obeying the same law of gravity, one of Nicky's sheets of plywood slides from its berth on the bar and slams to the floor with a resonant echo. Nicky vents what I can only assume is a Sicilian curse.

In the manager's office I try to explain things to Nan while she rummages through a pile of old clothes looking for something in my size. "I'm just stressed out because my boss is prepping me for this big proposal in Tucson in two weeks, and then my mom called me at work today, which she never does."

"What's in Tucson?" Nan has more clothes scattered around her office than I have hanging in my closet. A toothbrush peeks out from underneath a lacy sleeve.

"A big research firm that my boss wants to start using our software. If I do the presentation, and it goes well, it will clinch my promotion."

Without warning Nan flings open the office door and screams out of it. "*Nicky!* Could you keep it down out there?"

Nicky, who fears Nan in none of her tempers, hammers a board with significant emphasis. He's adding a platform behind the bar because he thinks if he looks taller, he'll get better tips. He's about as tall as a twelve-year-old, but his compact body is definitely that of a developed male, and he wears trousers tight enough to prove it. I throw my arms across my chest in pure reflex and Nan grins when she catches me doing it. "Nick won't ravish you. You're not his type. Too tall—too female."

"Cold," I defend myself, reaching for a paint-spattered T-shirt.

When I'm in a pair of her overalls, my hair pulled back and her old sneakers on my feet, we drape the floor and crack open the cans of base coat. Hiring painters is not an operational expense Nan can afford right now. Having been raised by a professional painter, I'm a whiz at all the basics, and Nan pays me back in free drinks.

"So," she says, setting up the stepladder, "what are you really upset about? Tucson, or Mom?"

"Mom." I love mixing paint, or even just stirring it, watching the smooth slopes fold in on one another. I try to lean over and take a sniff without Nan's noticing.

"Phone's ringing," Nicky announces, ignored.

"I saw that. I bet you sniffed glue when you were a kid, too." Nan throws me one of the nylon brushes. "What's the matter with Mom?"

I debate telling her, watching as she vaults up the ladder. It would embarrass my mother to know I was sharing tidbits about her health with my friends. Vivian blushes and changes the channel when advertisements for creams to treat yeast infections or vaginal itch come on the television. She won't even send my dad out to buy tampons, or, as she calls them, her lady's necessaries.

"She calls it a feminine complaint."

"Nan! Get your phone!" Nicky yells across the room.

"Feminine complaint? Oh, Lord," Nan says. I tip some paint into the roller pan and hand it up to her, and as I do, the pan tilts and institutional white slops over my hand. In surprise I let go. The pan falls and paint splashes everywhere. I let out a shriek that startles Nan.

"Chill out, sister. I told you it's water-based."

"Yeah, but it's a waste of paint." In the borrowed clothes I'm clumsy, heavy and thick.

"Nicky, throw us a bar rag, will you?" Nan hollers across the room, which is a span of no more than twenty feet, but Nick has stopped banging and started pounding.

"Is somebody going to answer the mother-loving phone?"

"It's not my phone," Nan yells back, catching the cloth in mid-air.

"It's my phone," I say, taking the washcloth from Nan, and Nicky dives into my purse with the quickness of a seal. Nan watches me for half a second, then grabs my arm and begins scrubbing with great energy. It amuses me when Nan gets motherly. I'm older than she is, but she believes she's much more worldly.

"What sort of feminine complaint are we talking about?" she wants to know.

"Oh, she's got this bleeding, and she doesn't want to go to the doctor. Isn't bleeding the type of thing that is supposed to make you *want* to go to the doctor?"

"Menopause," Nan announces. "It'll turn her into a raving bitch. Get ready."

"No, it's Nick," Nicky says from behind us. "Can I take a message?"

"That's what I thought, too. But she says she's been bleeding for a month now. I don't know why she hasn't told someone long before this."

Nicky's laugh sounds like a seal's too, the little barking kind. "No, she's not lying in bed while I feed her grapes! I said, she's got paint on her hands. She's helping Nan."

"Ben!" Nan bellows. "Tell him to get over here. He can do the ceiling."

"Okay, Nan says—Okay, so you know where—Okay, bye then," Nick ends, holding out the cell phone and looking at me. "He hung up on me."

"That's just Ben. He's very abrupt with his endings. Beginnings too, for that matter."

Nick hands the phone to me and I check the display. There's one missed call from Jeff. He must have tried me while I was out on the street and didn't hear the phone over the crashing of skyscrapers.

"Has she made an appointment?" Nan wants to know, turning back to her paint.

"We discussed it. I want her to and she doesn't. I may have become a little vehement."

"Tell her to come to Chicago. There are specialists here."

"Sure," Nicky offers. "We'll have mother's night specials at the bar."

We've got one wall almost done when the door to the street bangs open. It was propped open with a chair, so the banging is on purpose. Having announced himself with a long-legged kick, Ben slides in, singing like the vaudeville frog on the old Looney Tune shows.

Not even Nan is immune, though she tries to hide her smirk. "You're in a jolly mood."

"He's had his late afternoon coffee injection," I guess, assessing the java-jacketed cups in his hands. He sets two down on a table, nestling them between the upturned legs of a chair.

"Guess what the Institute just got at auction?" he demands. "And guess who gets to restore it?"

"Guess who cares?" is Nan's answer. "If you stay, you paint."

"Can't stay. Can't paint. Have to run home and change." He waggles his eyebrows suggestively at her, crossing the room to me.

"Hot date tonight?" Nan scoffs, while Nicky looks crestfallen.

"Yes and no. My friend's sister is in town and I promised I'd entertain her. Hey, you're cute in bibs," he says to me, dropping a quick kiss on my temple. At the same time he presses the coffee cup into my freshly scrubbed hand.

"Bring her by here," Nan says. "Bring all your friends."

"You won't be done by then." Ben eyes the wall, the crazy quilt-patch of paint samples and then the squeaky clean swath that we've just made.

"It's dark at night. Who will notice?" Nan wants to know.

"I'll know," Ben says. "Even if I can't see it, I'll know it's there. It will be like a big white eye just looking at me. Lucy, where will you be tonight?"

"Home, probably. Working." I wish I had plans. "What was it?"

"What was what?" He looks up from behind the bar, where Nicky is showing him the modifications. On the platform, Ben towers moreso than usual. Nicky flexes.

"The piece you got. The Art Institute got."

"I'm not telling you. I'm going to make it good as new, and then I'll show you." He gives me a one-armed hug before he leaves and throws a kiss at Nan. "Ciao, bambinos. Luce, if she's boring I'll call you so you can come rescue me, okay?"

With that, he whirls out the door, and Nick throws down his hammer. I turn my attention back to the wall. Nan's eyes drill little holes into the side of my face. I pretend I'm concentrating.

"So. You want to order a pizza?" she inquires.

"Not really. I need to get home eventually. Call my mom. Feed the fish."

"He's gay."

"I wish!" Nicky howls from the other side of the room.

"He's crazy," Nan says loyally.

"I'm the crazy one." I try to laugh. "Something would have happened by now, don't you think? I mean, if anything were going to happen? We've been friends for two years."

"Look at it this way." Her squeeze on my shoulder makes me feel like a dog that just got hit by a car. "If he screws up with other girls, there's always another girl. If he screws up with you, he's lost you. You're gone."

"Where would I go? You don't know how many times he's knocked on my door at two a.m. after some stupid date, and we stay up all night playing cards and watching Netflix, and he falls asleep in my bed—in my *bed*, mind you—and that's it. I don't know what I could say to him. Use it or lose it?"

"Hang out with us tonight," Nan says. "Blow him off. Let him see what it feels like."

"I can't." My fingers are flecked with white, like leprosy, as I seal the can of paint. "I have to talk some sense into my mother before she bleeds to death."

Nicky hugs me, firm and long, and I'm grateful even though he concludes with a squeeze on my behind. "It's not like you always think, Lucy," he says as if dispensing great wisdom. "Just because you pick up the pieces doesn't mean you get to keep them."

The next day, I suspect, is an eleven-incher. Things are getting violent. I throw a scarf around my neck and walk through parking lots so I don't have to cut beneath any skyscrapers. The wind hits clean and crisp in my face and I hope no one will notice if I close my eyes for just a second. I love Chicago in the fall, the way the buildings downtown make the streets a wind tunnel, the way it can take you half an hour to walk down to the lake and ten minutes to walk back.

My friends from college laughed at me when I told them I wanted to move to the big city. "New York's a big city," they said. "LA's a big city. Why compromise?"

"Iowa City is a big city," my mom said.

I've been to both coasts. I've had brief infatuations with Central Park and Santa Monica Pier, but I love the lift in the bottom of my stomach on the approach to O'Hare when my plane sweeps out over the lake, a deep blue shimmer scalloped at the edge with the tall buildings hemming the shore. I can wait two months for the latest self-help trend, the newest play, or the next burned-out chef to work its way to the heartland. Chicago still has a sense of humor.

The one time all day that my boss comes by my desk, I'm surfing the Internet. My phone rings right as he opens his mouth to comment. "No dysfunctional bleeding until after Tucson," he says, straight-faced. "I need you for this, Lucy."

Face on fire, I pick up the phone. It's Jeff. "Did you get my message?" he asks while my boss's back looms significantly near, the black-suited shoulders very square.

"Message? No." I watch as Donald mixes his coffee, one ear clearly tuned in to my conversation. "Text me. Can't talk right now. Terribly busy, Tucson and all."

The minute I hang up on him, my display buzzes again. "I called you six times last night," Ben fires at me the moment I answer. "What were you *doing?*"

"Research," I say. "I'll call you later, all right?"

"Do you even know how much bad karma you're generating? Do you care?"

"A regular switchboard in here, isn't it?" Donald observes, coffee in hand, interposing his black-suited shadow once more over my desk. "Tucson will be a nice break for you."

"You don't even want to *try* to meet the rent on my condo if you get me fired," I hiss into the phone as the black suit removes itself to its office.

This seems to mollify him. "Meet me at the Java Stop after work and I'll forgive you for blowing me off last night," Ben says nicely.

"I told Nan I'd help her paint."

"We'll both help her paint. Don't stand me up," he says, and hangs up on me.

'Dysfunctional bleeding,' my computer screen blinks at me. It lists common causes, symptoms, treatment. I think I know why my mother is afraid to go to the doctor. I close the site and pull up the Tucson proposal, hoping Donald will walk by again and catch me working.

Ben and I selected the Java Stop as our hang-out partly because it's halfway between our places, travel-time wise; I just walk up Ohio Street, and he comes from Lincoln Park on the El. Also, they have comfortable furniture. I teased him about the looks he gets from the counter girls until I realized that Ben really doesn't notice how often women look at him. He's addicted to the hazelnut house blend. I asked him once to name the one thing he couldn't live without and he answered, "Coffee."

The night I met Ben, we stayed up all night drinking coffee. We were other people's dates for a charity dinner held at the Tremont downtown. I was new to the city and a co-worker set me up with a friend of his. Ben was there with somebody who had been my co-worker's ex, or sister, or maybe second cousin; we tried to sort out the tangled network as we stood by the champagne fountain while our dates struck up a lively conversation with each other. For a while we made up dialogue for the other guests and floated boats made from folded napkins in the champagne, until we were asked to leave. When the hotel bar closed we headed to some cheap all-night diner where we drank pot after pot of truck stop coffee and revealed the entire history of our lives. When the morning shift arrived we stumbled out into a hazy dawn and flagged a taxi to my place.

"It's a palace," Ben said as we reeled gritty-eyed past the doorman, through the apartment complex, then through the courtyard fronting the smug interlaced row of townhouses, one of which belonged to me. "It's like a twelfth-century keep."

"Yeah, but without all the stinking moats and heads on stakes and stuff," I said.

Ben yawned against the doorframe while I unlocked my door and led the way upstairs to my flat, where he said, "What? No fish tank?" and then passed out on my couch. I crawled out of bed two hours later to the smell of pancakes and fresh coffee. When I scuffed in my slippers out to the kitchen, Ben grinned at me and pointed with the spatula towards the bag of oranges and two large to-go cups sitting on the table.

"I went to the deli round the corner and got us the daily dose. How do you survive without a coffee maker? Is yours broken?"

"I'm more of a hot cocoa person," I said, peeking beneath a lid.

He shook his head. "I knew there had to be something wrong with you."

Ben spent the whole afternoon at my place, rifling through my CD collection and my bookcases, listening to the detailed account of my severance with my long-time boyfriend Richard and sharing advice from his experiences with serial dating. Ben and I never had a warming-up period; we collided like atoms, the bond immediate and unexplained. I've seen him through three jobs, his father's remarriage, and more flings than he or I can count. He's steered me through one promotion, two breakups, and all of my fights with my mother. I don't know what I'd do without him. The absence of Ben in my life would loom larger than the presence of anyone else.

Ben comes into the coffee shop wearing his green turtleneck sweater and beat-up jeans, his glasses on and his brown hair sticking up in tufts that certain hairdressers strive to emulate and which Ben achieves by simply not combing. Other patrons pause in their conversations and turn to look at him. Ben has the magnetic field of a small planet.

As soon as I tell him about my mother, he insists on calling her. Ben adores Vivian. Vivian wants me to bring Ben to Iowa City so she can bake him muffins and he can go to the junkyard with my father looking for old furniture.

I grouch at him while he scans the contacts on my cell phone. "As if she doesn't have enough to worry about."

"I'd hang up on you too. You were a crank when I called you at work."

"Only because Donald had already caught me surfing medical websites. Not activity that is going to earn me a big bonus."

"It's just menopause," Ben diagnoses, touching the screen. "My mother went through it a couple years ago. Irregular bleeding for a time, and then it stops altogether."

"I was on the website that said cysts," I tell him. "I was on the website that said cancer."

He gives me a stern look. "Don't do that. You'll just upset Vivian."

I refill my hot chocolate at the counter while he leaves a message. I return to narrowed eyes and an accusing stare. "Your display says Jeff called. What does he want?"

"Alas, not me. Probably his movie. I kept his VHS of *Arsenic and Old Lace*."

"Let's tape over it with that World War II tanker special the History Channel is running."

"How about reruns of *I Love Lucy*?"

"Oh, very good," Ben approves. "I've taught you well."

"My mom wants me to move back home," I blurt out as I sink onto the couch. I hate how the sudden falling silence in the room makes that statement sound so much larger and desperate than it really is. "She says I could study art history at the university."

Ben lifts my feet into his lap and uses my legs to prop open Sunday's newspaper.

"Why would you?" he asks, skimming through Lifestyles without looking up. "You have a great apartment. You have a career. She just wants you to marry Richard and bear grandchildren that she can bounce on her knee."

"Richard's no longer available. He's had a new girlfriend for a while now. Betty, or something like that."

"I envy men like Richard," Ben says, flipping through Lawn & Garden. "I never have relationships. I have brief, violent spasms of attachment that end in humiliation on the part of one party and eventual disgust on the part of the other."

"That's a good title for a memoir, isn't it? *Love and Other Natural Disasters*." I hold my mug of hot chocolate between both hands, letting the steam curl beneath my chin. Paul Simon sounds tinnily from the speakers.

"Why not *Life As I Know It?*" Ben says. "That's really all you're writing about."

"I'm going to write a chapter where Jeff dies of grief over how he treated me. A sort of *Dangerous Liaisons* kind of thing. I think it would help me be less bitter."

"Wasn't he with Nan before he was with you?" Ben observes from the paper. "And didn't he start pursuing you while he was still with her? He is not a man sensitive to guilt."

"You men never are." It's a cheap shot, but pure reflex.

"Don't say 'you men' like that. Don't put me in the lineup with Jeff."

I can feel my shins falling asleep, but to move my legs would be to apologize. "Why not? You both have the basic equipment."

"But the difference is, I have the upgrade package with sensitivity and distinction. Jeff is your basic unimaginative male slut."

I have to stare. "Don't tell me your little friend went home alone last night."

"She most certainly did. I sent her back to her little gumball machine where she belongs. I am weary of the ten-second gumball buzz. I want the banquet, with cocktails first and coffee after dessert."

Watching the side of Ben's face, the cheekbones that could cut glass and the straight, square, gorgeous chin, I am sure the lack of interest had been one-sided. The night I met him, I spent the whole first hour of our conversation staring at his eyes, watching them change from gold to green to brown, as facile as his moods.

"What if Vivian's right? What if I do need to put down roots? I am living without soil. I lead a hydroponic existence."

Ben picks up the Travel pages and starts thumbing through them. "How economical of you. Soil is so messy. Why deal with it if you can dissolve all the necessary nutrients into water? Then you can move wherever the whim takes you. Would you like to go to San Francisco?" He flashes me a picture of the sea lions sunning themselves at Pier 39.

"The chapter about you is going to be called Changing the Subject," I tell him, taking a long sip of hot cocoa, whipped cream sticking to my upper lip.

"Is that all I am to you? A chapter?"

"What more did you expect?"

"I want to be a theme," Ben says. "I want to be a recurring motif."

I call home the evening after my mother's doctor appointment, which I scheduled for her. I am adept at nagging, having learned from the best. When the receptionist at the clinic heard her symptoms, she booted an annual pelvic to fit my mother in.

"So, how did it go?"

"I got an early seed catalogue in the mail today," she reports. "I'm going to start planning my garden for the spring."

"I mean, what did the doctor say?"

"Oh, and you'll never guess who I ran into this morning!"

I don't even think of him until she says his name. "Richard?" I am truly surprised. "Where'd you see him?"

They are only small things: they were at the grocery store. Her name is Becky. They were tan and smiling and had just been diving in the Bahamas. They're getting married in June. My mother gave Becky my address so she can send me an invitation. None of this should come as a surprise; I know it's Becky who sits at the patio table with him, a bottle of merlot gleaming like rain-dark earth. I know they prop themselves up with fat pillows on the bed on Sunday afternoons while she sips hot chocolate and he reads to her from the paper. She's the one who cradles his head on her lap as he falls asleep during yet another movie. As it should be.

"You should see the rock on her finger," my mom exclaims. "It's the size of a pea."

I can't answer. Something a bit larger than a pea has formed in my throat.

"Still, you're much prettier than she is," my mother says. "She's got this nose."

I can picture Becky in a wedding gown, and I have to agree her face would look a little round under the veil. But she is perfect for Richard, really, both of them smoothed out and smiling and stuffed on the inside like chocolate éclairs. I try to imagine introducing Ben to a tuxedoed Richard, stout and with his hair thinning, and I can't picture even a corsaged and married Richard standing out next to tall, lean, caustic Ben. Snooping through a photo album of mine, Ben discovered the picture Richard had given me of himself in his National Guard uniform.

"This?" he had exclaimed. "*This* is the man whose heart you broke?"

"I didn't break his heart."

Ben held the photo next to my face and looked at it, then at me, then back to smiling, blue-eyed Richard.

"Oh yes you did. You crushed him."

"You wouldn't know."

"Any other girl in the world would stay in Iowa City with him and start increasing the tax base as soon as possible. And he picks the girl who decides he has no passion and moves to the big, exciting, soulless city."

"Oh, and I have more news," my mother says.

Ben calls the instant I hang up the phone. I wander to the fish tank, wonder if I fed them yet, and toss in a few flakes while I debate answering.

"I'm at the Bongo Bar with some people from work," he reports. "What are you doing?"

"Making phone calls. Looking for something to eat. There is no food at *all* in this apartment." I slam the refrigerator door shut.

"Not pleasant phone calls, if the gauge on your temper is at the level I'm reading."

"Vivian has to get a hysterectomy." I sit down at my kitchen table, prop the phone against my shoulder with my chin, and spread my hands over the scuffed tabletop. I lay my fingers against the knife scars, trying to fit my knuckles against the crooks.

"Can't they just put her on estrogen therapy? That's what my mom did."

"Apparently the symptoms are too severe. The ultrasound showed cysts on her ovaries."

"The benign fibroid sort of cysts, right?" The background noise from his end grows quiet suddenly; he's moved away. Only Ben would know this much about the mature female reproductive body.

"No." I swallow hard. "The non-benign kind. Her doctor wants to take everything out."

"When?"

"Next Tuesday." The table top feels cold beneath my fingers. "I rented a car for Sunday. I'm going to drive out there and stay as long as she needs. Donald is going to have a fit that I can't do Tucson. No promotion for me." I purposely called the office voicemail rather than his cell to leave a message on the chance I would break down at using the words "mother" and "surgery" in the same sentence.

"Christ. Vivian," Ben says softly.

I have found tracks for all my fingers on my right hand but not all the fingers on my left. Behind me, the fish tank burps as a bubble goes through the filter hose.

"People don't die from hysterectomies, do they?"

"Of course not," Ben says. "It never happens. It's just a routine surgery nowadays. Like an appendectomy."

"The doctor said he doesn't like to do total hysterectomies unless he really has to."

"Do you really have no food there?"

"Not even olives. I ate them all last night when I was watching *Breakfast at Tiffany's*."

"Come meet me at Sergio's. I'll stuff you with olives and take you to the French feature at the Esquire. I think they're showing *La Femme Nikita*. You need it, after Jeff.*"

"Know what else? Richard's getting married. I found that out today, too."

A short, pooled silence, and then, "Wear your sexiest outfit. I'm going to take you out and get you roaring drunk."

At Sergio's we haggle over French burgundy or Napa Valley merlot. The sommelier favors the burgundy and I win. "Let's drink to Richard," Ben suggests after he pours the wine.

"You're cruel." One sip and I've already spilled on my shirt.

"I'm not. You wish him all the best. You're glad you won't be the one who has to wash his dirty socks for the rest of your life."

"Who's going to wash my socks?" I want to know, spearing the black olives off his salad.

Ben raises his glass and examines the wine. I imagine the deep red is the color of our vital organs, the color of oxygenated arteries. The color of a womb.

"Do you know who I'm going to marry?" he says. "A woman I can talk to. I figure when I'm eighty pretty much everything else will be limp, but my mind will be going strong. I want to sit and chat with the little woman while we play backgammon or rummy and have her laugh at my jokes."

I look at the flat space where my plate had been, a few dabbles of dressing dotting the tablecloth in exactly the shape of a Valentine heart. "As long as her mind is gone by then, she will," I say, but I hardly mean it.

After coffee and dessert we catch the El to Oak Street and the Esquire. Beneath a grated staircase a woman stands preaching to a small group of people waiting in line for tickets at the automat. A captive audience, most ignore her; some listen, nodding in encouragement.

"God made this world," the woman shouts. She has frizzy braids and wears a sweater and an Indian-print skirt, no stockings, and a pair of black combat boots. The skirt whips around her legs, lifted by the fall wind. "All the plants, all the animals, every rock and tree. God made you. The color of your hair, every cell in your body. This was all God's idea."

"Did you hear that?" I ask Ben. "This was all God's idea. I'm going to tell Vivian that."

His hand on mine tightens as he glances down at me. "Everything's going to be okay, Lucy."

Ben's saying that makes me feel as I do when my father tells me everything is going to be all right: it's crossing home plate, touching the safety zone in a game of tag. I want to curl up against the hard door of his chest and sleep there, out of the wind.

"Do you know I heard this story once about orphanages in Victorian England?" I tell him. "The infant mortality rate was incredibly high. They had food, shelter, and were relatively free from disease, but no one could understand why these babies didn't thrive."

"Why didn't they?"

"They were never touched. They were fed and given blankets and that was it. No one held them, or cuddled them, or anything."

"Poor little tykes," Ben says.

"People die for lack of love," I say. I believe this.

We cut out of the movie early to head to the Bongo Bar. Ben's friends are still there, and I want to talk to Nan. Business is booming; every available inch is crammed with bodies and a haze drifts over the heads of the crowd, a combination of cigarette smoke and poorly ventilated desperation. In the dim light you can't tell that the wall is half-painted. Ben's friends crowd around one of the tables by the window. A fake redhead in a low-cut V-neck, whose name I can never recall because she never speaks to me, squeals at the sight of Ben and pulls him into a chair next to her. I head to the bar where Nicky is gleaming in a tight white shirt and industrious sweat.

"What'll it be, beautiful?"

"The strongest thing you can think of," I say, and watch while he shakes and pours a martini for another customer in a motion so smooth it's almost sexual. I've seen Nicky practice his moves afternoons before the bar opens and I have to admit that if I didn't know better, I'd be giving him my phone number, too.

"Ben's got a millipede attached to him," he observes, glancing over at the art table.

"Ben's on his own. I've had it. I'm moving back to Iowa City."

"For real?" He doesn't pause in his slide from one liquor bottle to another. "What about Nan? What about me?"

"I might not be serious. I don't know. But I'm going home next week, and if I lose my job over this, I'm not coming back."

"For you." With a flourish he places a foaming glass before me, and then lays a toothpick full of olives over the edge. "A Bongo Banger. Nicky's own."

"I'm taking a poll," I tell him after the first sip. "Tell me the one thing you can't live without. And don't say sex," I warn him as he grins. "That's off the list. You're talking to a desperate woman."

"I could help you out with that," he says with a wink.

I nearly choke on my Bongo Banger. "That would be my first gay man."

"Make Ben jealous." His eyes twinkle under the bar lights. "Maybe that's what he needs."

"I'm afraid Ben doesn't operate in the normal male mode. The window of opportunity has pretty much slammed shut at this point."

I make the mistake of looking back at the table. Ben's head is bent as he listens to the girl next to him. She reaches out and puts her hand on his forearm.

"Hey, where're you going?" Nicky wants to know.

"Where's Nan?"

"In the office. But I wouldn't go in there if I—"

I painted the door to the manager's office red, a bold red, while Nan was out one day. She loved it. She painted a dark crescent moon on it at eye-level. When I fling the door open I can hear a *whoosh* of surprise. The desk lamp is dimmed, and it takes a moment for my eyes to make out shapes. Nan with knees straddled wide sits on her desk, skirt peeled to her waist, hands braced. And Jeff, in *flagrante delicto*, moving against her, jeans drooping. Their heads swivel in my direction with a mechanical slowness. The three of us stand in tableau for a long minute, me at the apex of both their gazes, lit up as brilliantly as the Hotel Inter-Continental.

"Oh, hello. Is this the line? How long is the wait?"

"Lucy," Nan says, her face registering shock. "Sweetie. Don't jump to conclusions."

"So was I before or after on the call list?" I ask Jeff. "I'm just curious. Did you call me because you couldn't get hold of Nan, or did you come here when you couldn't get hold of me?"

"Bastard," Nan exclaims as she starts rolling off the desk, and I hope she isn't talking to me. Nicky calls to me as I shoot out the door, but I plow straight through the crowd to the table where Ben and his friends are having a jolly time.

"Hello," I announce to the room at large. "I'm leaving."

Ben tries to scramble to his feet and the redhead clamps onto his arm. "What? Did I miss something? What's going on?"

"I'm going now." I'm speaking into the formidable bosom of the redhead, who has interposed herself between us. "I'll call you from Iowa City." I push my way outside through the crowd of people waiting to get in, until the leather and heels and dyed hair let me go and I spill out onto the sidewalk.

The worst part is, not a single person runs out the door after me.

My cab driver's name is Kim. The photo on the ID hanging from the visor grins hideously, like a disembodied head.

"Do you know anyone who ever had a hysterectomy?" I ask him.

"Oh, yeah, yeah, my cousin once. It was really bad. The thing busted in him and flooded all over and he had to go to the emergency room and almost died. Very messy, very bad."

"Wow," I say, "I hope he's all right now." I leave him a ten dollar tip.

I asked Nan my question that afternoon as we put the finishing touches on the sunflowers. "The one thing I can't live without?" She sounded amused. "Is this some kind of survey?"

"Human interest only."

"What have you got so far?"

"Food, sex, love. For some, religion. For others, art."

"You know what I say?" she reported, pulling at a black curl. "I say air."

"Air," I repeated.

"You know it, baby. You can go seven days without food, three days without water, but without breathing? Three minutes tops."

"I heard some Olympic swimmers can go five minutes holding their breath."

"I went skydiving once," Nan said. She gave a neon sunflower a smiley face. "It was the most incredible sensation you can imagine. Every nerve in your body comes alive. It's like you're floating—or flying, like in dreams. It's like the only reason you're up is that there's nothing holding you down."

I am not sleeping but sitting in the dark watching the fish when I hear the clatter against my window. I open the door to the balcony and step outside. In the courtyard the night air is cold but soothing, like swimming in mountain water. Ben is bent over in the bushes.

"Are you throwing up or looking for more rocks to throw at my window?"

"I tried calling you," he says too loudly, straightening. "I kept getting your voice mail."

"I was busy."

"Are you alone?"

"Of course I'm alone," I hiss at him. "Do you mind not waking up the whole building?"

"Where's Jeff?"

"He wouldn't dare come here. Even if he wanted to."

"Nan tried calling you too. She wants you to know she's not with him, it was strictly sex." The lamplights glint off his glasses, hiding his eyes.

I shrug. "I'm just glad I get to keep the movie."

"Who were you talking to, then?"

"I was on the Internet. Looking at medical websites. None of your business. Are you drunk?"

"I don't think so. Maybe."

Ben never gets drunk. I look down at the shape of him, standing in the bushes beneath my balcony, and have that funny sensation I get when I'm sitting in the chair at the optometrist's and he's flipping the lenses in front of my eyes. "One, or two," he drones on, over and over, "one, or two," and everything just gets blurrier and blurrier. But then he hits on the right lens and things snap into place, so clear and obvious they make the eyes ache.

"Nobody," Ben says after a pause, "but *nobody* who gets a degree in art history ever makes any money. I stand to know, damn you."

That *damn you* thrills me. It's so unlike Ben. I curl my hands around the iron bar of the balcony, a sharp cold hardness beneath my palms. To my right the yellow moon burns a hole in the sky, and to the left the sodium lights gleam off the glass wall holding back the swimming pool.

"I don't believe in strictly sex, you know," I say at last.

"Of course not," Ben says. "You just end up with a guy like Jeff, who's never been to an art show in his life."

When I was a kid, and bored, I made telephones out of two tin cans and a piece of string and pestered my mom until she played with me. She wouldn't stop what she was doing, knitting or stirring peas on the stove, but she'd crook my phone against her ear and talk to me while I stood around the corner in the hallway and whispered into the can. That was how I told her all my secrets. When I ran out of conversation or imagination, I'd end with saying, OK, I love you.

"OK," I say to Ben. "Do you want a jacket if you're going to stand there all night?"

"Aren't you going to let me in?"

In a moment of utter stillness we stand staring at each other. Blocks away, the lights atop the Hancock building blip in tandem, off and on, in their own gentle and faultless rhythm. The Hancock building will never tip over. They thought of that in advance and designed the sides to narrow near the top, giving it a square alien head with flashing antennae. On its immoveable base the Hancock could sit there forever, blinking, battered by the great winds.

"No, I'm not going to let you in." In the night breeze I could be a runaway, I could be an owl about to lift off into flight. "I'm tired of the á la carte menu. I want the banquet, too."

Behind the glasses Ben's eyes gleam like a dark sea. Deliberately, he grabs the bottom rung of the balcony, a challenge. I stare back at him, feeling cold air on my knees. He pulls himself up in a few easy movements and clears the railing and lands on the balcony like water falling into a glass jar, and I stand in the doorway watching him come to me.

If it happened any other way, of course, it would have been ridiculous. If he said anything, I wouldn't believe him. If he reached for me in my kitchen, pressing my back into the oven handle on the stove, I'd have socked him. But right here on my balcony he walks up to me and puts his hand on the back of my neck and pulls me against him, and the shamelessness of being in plain view, the simple urgency of being reached for on an open balcony makes the air around us come alive. A champagne buzz goes all through me. It's better than skydiving. It's better than anything. Until this moment of Ben's mouth opening on mine I hadn't known that I stopped breathing a very, very long time ago.

The phone rings a few hours later. A dim light eases through the window. My groping hand knocks a book off the nightstand and, I think, Ben's glasses.

"I've decided on orchids," my mother announces.

I glance at Ben to see if the phone woke him. He hasn't moved.

"I'm going to raise orchids. They need temperature control, of course, but your dad can build a greenhouse for me out back. He says he wouldn't mind."

"Orchids are a lot of work, Mom," I say, keeping my voice low. I try to slide out of bed and, quick as a snake, Ben's warm arm clamps around me.

"I don't see why I couldn't give it a try," Vivian says. "They have pictures in the plant catalog of the houses you can build. We'll heat it and put in lights."

I poke Ben in the side and he groans, then rolls over, freeing me. I pull on shorts and a tank top and sit in my bedroom window. It has a wide sill and looks out at the courtyard, with a broad view to the north. In the east, above the fat squat block of the apartment building, I can see thin threads of color poking their way around the city skyline. In the spaces the lake gleams like mercury.

"I suppose I might kill a few of them on my first try," she starts, but I don't want her to anticipate disappointment.

"I'll help you pick out seedlings when I'm home. We'll start with the easy ones."

"It's a two-year Master's of Arts degree," she says softly. "You'll do sculpture, painting, architecture, everything. You can specialize in Western art."

Sitting on my windowsill I feel like a wild woman, cool wood pressing against my back, morning air on my bare skin. I picture my mother standing in her kitchen next to the green countertop, phone tucked against her ear, one hand on the glossy pages of her plant magazine and the other on her stomach, trying to sense where the tumors are growing, imagining them in 3-D, the shape of peaches, glowing orange against the deep shadowed cavern of her insides.

Sometimes, during the telephone game, I'd come around the corner and stand behind her, swooping my arms. Can you see me? I'd demand. Can you see me waving at you? She'd peer into the tin can, squint one eye. Why, I can! she'd say. What a big wave!

"I love you, Vivian Marie," I whisper into my end of the phone.

"Well," she says after a while. "I suppose we don't have all the museums and architecture and such here. And you wouldn't be making as good a salary."

"Who'd make sure you don't kill all your orchids?"

"Oh, hush," she says. "Your dad will help me. We'll be all right."

Ben, sprawled across my bed, one foot hanging over the edge, sleeps like a little boy, his lower lip tucked in a pout. My mother is alone in her kitchen but somewhere upstairs, behind her, my father snores in warm oblivion. The thing is, I like my job. There are art classes offered at the Institute. I love my apartment and the way the heater in the pool room whirs like helicopter blades in the winter. I love the glitter of Michigan Avenue, a roaring crowd in Wrigley Field, standing on Navy Pier with water on every side. There are a dozen ways the conversation with Ben could go, of course. But I want to believe that later I will run to the deli for coffee and oranges, maybe eggs and cheese for an omelet, and we will smirk at each other across my scarred kitchen table with the *Sun-Times* between us and this deep bronze color polishing the sky.

"Look out your window right now, Mom. I'm waving at you."

She chuckles softly. "The airport tower is blocking my view."

Of all the things I could say—*I'm coming home. We'll take it day by day. Everything is going to be all right*, though that's my dad's line—I want to tell her that I wasn't running. Nothing about my life so far has been wrong.

And I do want her to meet Ben. I want her to look at me behind his back and say, "Richard who? I was so wrong, darling."

But I don't say anything. We just sit there breathing, her breath and mine into the tin cans and the tight knitted cord between us, with Ben's steady breath in the bed behind me, and I watch the sun rising over the skyscrapers, lightly, swaying like a balloon rising into the atmosphere, like the first swelling notes of a song.

FICUS

"It's true," the woman said. "I think I'm ready."

She crossed her legs at the ankle. She touched the handles of her heavy shoulder bag and then patted her knee, like she was putting something into place. The light material of her trousers felt smooth and cool beneath her fingers. Like snakeskin.

"Yes," the doctor said. "I understand how you might feel that way."

He was wearing a light blue polo shirt. His khaki slacks had long lost their manufactured crease and his brown loafers were scuffed and beginning to crack at the toes, the seam coming apart at the heel. The woman noticed these sorts of things, though she did not make moral judgments about them. He was losing his hair and, to hide this, he brushed a few long strands over the top of his head. His glasses were spotty with dust. He carried cheap ballpoint pens that he picked up at random places, a new one in his chest pocket each week. He sat in a dark leather swivel chair, but he never swiveled.

"Have you ever been to Puerto Rico?" she asked.

"I have not." The doctor looked down at his clipboard and made a few notes on it with a blue ballpoint pen. He wrote, as the woman had learned in one of their first meetings, in a shorthand he himself had invented. A phonetic language, something Henry Higgins might use. He had a black pen in his chest pocket and a green one tucked behind his ear.

"I think I'll enjoy it," the woman said. "I'm renting a car."

"I wish you had talked with me about this," the doctor said. "It's important that you understand your intentions."

The woman nodded and smoothed the trouser material over her knee. This time he had left the blinds open on the window, and the late afternoon sun gently dispensed a copper gleam over the hardwood floor, the dusty desk, the ficus in the corner. The ficus didn't grow because, the woman knew, the doctor often failed to water it. She was sure that the ficus had looked exactly the same in all the time she had been coming here, almost three years. Sometimes its leaves, too, were spotty with dust, and sometimes it seemed that the cleaning lady thought to spray it down with her mister. The woman had been learning to pay attention and she knew now how to look for these things.

The doctor clicked and unclicked the blue plastic pen. "Let's set a time to meet when you come back, shall we? I don't want to lose any of the ground that we've made."

The woman stroked the material of her trousers with soft hands, over and over. She gave him a kind smile. This, too, was something she had learned over the last three years. When she had first come to this office, her smile was nervous. Then, for a long time, she had not smiled at all, and the doctor had to ask his secretary to bring in another tissue box. But they had grown comfortable together over time, nesting into this office, with the carpet she was sure was only cleaned once a year.

"I won't be coming back, I don't think," she said to the doctor.

He clicked the pen with a couple of violent starts. He looked directly at her. "You're staying in Puerto Rico?"

"I don't think," the woman said, "that I will be coming back *here*."

She smiled at him, waiting for approval. His reaction horrified her. He gripped both sides of his notepad with his hands. He stared hard at the paper, his own scrawled notes. Red spots appeared above the grey-salted stubble on his cheeks.

"You can't stop now," the doctor said. "You'll ruin everything."

Around the corner of the doctor's office, in the corner of the city park, a fountain had been installed a few years ago. The synthetic stones looked weathered like real rocks, and the embankment had been built to resemble a real waterfall, with reedy moss and everything. Many times she sat by this fountain and noticed that the fish in the pool were gone, and then, a few weeks later, they were back, minnow-sized. She didn't know where the water came from and she didn't know how it got recycled from the pool and piped back to the top, if it were ever cleaned, if it were ever tested, who fixed the plumbing when it was broken, who fed the fish. It was something that just kept functioning on its own, through a kind of invisible aid.

Many times, after she picked up her bag and came into the building and took the elevator to the fifth floor to sit down in this office, she felt she was still sitting outside on the rim of stone, hearing the low whirr and splash of that fountain. It would take many more years to figure out the mystery of it: not why it was there, or who tended it, or who made the water return over and over, but why someone had designed the false rocks and the false stones and piped in the aseptic water to try to create a waterfall that looked real.

The thing in her chest gave a little painful gulp. A bubble moved through her stomach. The woman hoped, with a sort of agony, that he could not hear it.

"I need to do this." She picked up her shoulder bag. "Please understand."

In all three years, he had never tried to touch her. He avoided touching her, drawing back when she walked into the office, handing her the tissue box with the business end canted towards her. Each time she left, they nodded agreeably at each other, she standing with her hand on the door, he placing both hands on his desk, on either side of his notepad. But suddenly, when she stood, he stretched out a hand toward her. It hung in the space between them like a hyphen.

She looked at his hand. His fingers were short and pudgy. The nails had been bitten off. Slight dark hairs covered the skin between his knuckles. The woman looked up at him. That bubble moved through her chest again.

"I'm going," she said. She held her bag before her, across her chest.

"I'll mark you in my appointment book," the doctor said, leaving his hand there, attached to nothing. "The Tuesday after you return. The usual time. 3:15."

"Oh, Daniel," she whispered.

At the door, she wavered. She almost said, *Okay*. She hadn't realized. She hadn't thought she would feel like a murderer, like she was stabbing him in the chest with his pen. She had hoped, right up until this moment, that she was wrong about his need for her. Hoped she was not and never had been the reason that the ficus never grew. Had not wanted to admit that the water in that fountain repeated and recycled because of her, because she kept pumping it, kept it sterile, kept killing the fish.

I wish it could be different, she almost said. But then she saw his eyes.

"3:15," he repeated. "Two weeks from now." The finger with its knuckle pressing the pen had turned white.

Her voice sounded as if it came from elsewhere, behind her. "3:15," she said, and shut the door.

The city block was noisy and smelled of exhaust. The sun filtered through tiny granules of dust, and garbage skittered across the street. She thought of the sunny pictures in the guidebooks about Puerto Rico, of the smiling hotel keepers, the happy, tanned, model tourists reclining on a dizzying white beach. She wished she were really going there. It would mean that their three years had meant something. That at the last minute, after all they had been through together, after her terrible and exhausting and transformative journey, she had not emerged as someone who would lie to him. But sometimes it was simply too terrible to know the truth.

She turned away from the park and moved toward the city center, away from the fountain, away from the tourism office with its sultry pictures. For the first time in a long time, she wanted something real.

TANDEM

The jumpmaster, Travis, hitched the strap around my waist and buckled. His hand brushed my hip.

"Tighter," I said.

"That's tight."

Brandon said, "Mom."

"Check his." He was taller than me now. The goggles made his eyes buggy and bewildered. As a boy he sat on my feet while I cooked dinners, running his police cars along my calves. He had afternoon stubble and a divot in his eyebrow from that bolt on the swingset when he was five.

"This is the love of my life," I said. "You hear me? And it's his birthday."

Travis scanned him, yanking the straps that swaddled his jumpsuit. "Happy birthday," he said.

"Thirty hours of labor. Doctor put him in my hands and I said, that's the love of my life. In front of his father, too."

Travis nodded and said, "Just keep your feet together."

"She'll get it once we land," Brandon said. "It's going to be fine, mom. You'll love it."

"No, I won't, but I said I'd do it." I twined my fingers around my harness, thin straps of fabric and thread.

Travis hooked his carabiner to my belt and said, "3116."

"What?"

"Jumps."

I looked at the pack strapped to him. It didn't look big enough to hold safety, to cradle two human lives back to earth.

"So this is 3117?"

"3116. I always count the jump coming."

"That doesn't count. You can't count it until you land."

"Five," Brandon said, bracing his legs. He looked so much like his father, the hair, the shoulders. But he thought more like me.

I glanced out the window, the earth sliding beneath us.

"One." I heaved out the word.

"Let go," Travis said, looking at our hands.

The plane roared and tilted, in my chest the lightness of escape, then lift.

"I'll never let go," I said, and unlocked my fingers.

Travis reached across me and jerked the cord, unleashing Brandon's chute.

"Geronimooo!" Brandon threw himself into the tunnel of light, howling and fearless as the day he tore out of me.

And as I have every day since, I threw myself after.

We leapt together, and the sky caught us.

BAY CITY

The trouble began when Blanche jumped out of the convertible at the first wayside. It was Parker's fault; neither Simon nor I cared for boiled peanuts, but Parker considered that she needed a North Florida souvenir. Just when the back of her dark neat head clipped off underneath the orange welcome sign, Blanche the dog sailed out of the backseat, skidded across the shiny red trunk, and launched herself onto the pavement, nails chipping against the blazing hot asphalt as she beelined to the woods.

"Blanche! Baby!" Simon scrambled. His flailing hand caught a chunk of my ponytail and pinned my head to the headrest as he levered himself out of the backseat. I yodeled with pain. "Get her, Dana! She might go on the road! She might see a squirrel!"

I rubbed my head and stayed where I was: Blanche, being Simon's dog, was Simon's problem, and it was too humid to move. The late May sun shone like a heat lamp on unhatched eggs. Sweat slid sticky fingers over my collarbones and down my shoulder blades, pooling inside the built-in bra of my halter top. I coiled my hair off my neck and wished we were back on the highway, weaving in and out of the canopied shade. I should tell Parker to buy an alligator belt for Ivan. It might cause him to re-evaluate some of his choices. The sight of Simon, over six feet tall and skinny as string, darting between the wispy pines as he lured his wayward terrier back to him, only confirmed what I suspected: Before this weekend was over, we would all be very tired.

"The Flash once again saves the day," I said as Simon marched to the car, one bony hand clamped on Blanche's collar. The skintight, sleeveless red T-shirt with the Dykes in the City logo that I'd bought him for his birthday clashed outrageously with the dyed carrot-juice color of his hair and the orange-tinted sunglasses.

"You're a big help." He patted Blanche's wiry coat. This strange creature had squinched-up eyes and piebald spots where it looked like children had pulled out tufts of white fur. Simon loved her more than he loved anything on earth, more than he loved his ex. "You have no idea what Matt would do to me if I lost his dog."

"He's half your dog," I reminded him, and then felt pressed to add, "None of this was my idea."

"Parker's a cutie," Simon said by way of retribution. He propped his booted feet on Parker's headrest, shedding pine needles onto her seat. He'd made me drive his father's tomato-red Mustang first because Simon can't operate a standard transmission and second because he had a bright mental picture in his head wherein he reclined breezily in the backseat with Blanche as we roared down the highway to Bay City, sand kicking up behind us, Spanish moss swaying in our careless wake. He kept asking Parker and me to tie scarves over our hair.

"Parker's not my type," I said. I laid my arm along the top of the driver's door. The metal burned a smart strip of bacon across my forearm. I pulled my arm away.

"But Ivan's type, clearly." Simon smirked.

I curled my toes into my flip flops and studied the plastic flowers. I wondered what Ivan was doing back in their second-floor apartment, the smug blue door firmly shut, the lock scuffed with key marks from the nights they stumbled home together, drunk, hands beneath one another's clothes. I wondered what Corey was doing back at our apartment: if she'd already stripped off her clothes and gone to her studio, getting high on the smell of turpentine and paint, or if she was going through the mess we'd made, throwing out my things or cutting them apart for her sculptures. I'd had the forethought to pack all my favorite articles of clothing in my luggage, now nestled safely in the Mustang's trunk.

"I don't want Ivan," I said, "and that's a fact."

"What about Ivan?"

Parker stood poised at the passenger door, dressed in stylish black from the sunglasses and tailored trousers to the black sweater cardigan and the black mesh bag. She had no premonition about anything; I'd seen that from the moment Ivan brought her out to the car, a small huddled piece of coal, a black smudge next to the towering Adonis that was Ivan, with his profile meant for a Roman coin, a man a woman just might let ravish her if he burst into her hut waving a big sword, damn our treacherous biology. Two years ago he'd ended up next to me, yes me, at our graduate orientation class. I let him talk about the genius of Raymond Chandler and film noir and how graphic novels really are art, and from then on it was the two of us at the department parties and lectures and events, sharing a cheese plate and always the same hors d'oeuvres, he confiding about Jersey and his father and his fickle ex as though I could not reach out as gently as any girl to brush the crumbs of cracker from his mouth. And then in October, right before the Halloween party, the talk of Parker, who was so cool, so funny and smart and misunderstood, really misunderstood, like him; how fierce and wonderful, they could be misunderstood together.

Yes, Parker was innocent; subtext sheared over her head like a rain cloud, never touching a hair of her smart bob. She walked like a ballerina, rolling through her feet, arches so high you could play croquet through them. And Ivan wanted this, a little girl, a twirling top of a girl, a bright bagged black sweater of a girl. A fifth-year BFA in interior design, mother of God.

"I was just saying I can't believe Ivan wants to teach high school math," Simon said easily, moving his feet from Parker's headrest to the rim of his door. "I had him pegged for the literary arts."

"He has a white board at home. He solves theorems for fun," Parker said. She slipped into the passenger seat, a clothes hanger, an ink blot, flicking the seat belt across her chest. She had no breasts to speak of, a waist curved like a spoon. She placed her bag near her feet, primly zippered into black leather boots. I looked again: three-inch heels narrowing to a pencil point. Lethal.

"Here, puppy, sweetie pie," she said, turning and holding out a strip of beef jerky for Blanche. The dog, wheezing in the heat, snapped up the treat and shook her head wildly back and forth. A spatter of saliva hit the back of my neck. Simon's lip curled.

"Simon, what is it you study?" Parker asked politely while I started the car.

"Education Specialist, school of Psychology. Third year," he added, just to clarify his superior status to Ivan and me, the second-years.

"And Dana, you—?"

"I'm switching to an M.S. in marriage and family therapy," I said.

"Liar. You're getting an education leadership Ph.D. Whatever the hell that is."

"Seatbelts, please." I glared at his orange-shielded eyes in the rearview mirror. Parker took a boiled peanut out of the paper bag, neatly slid open the softened shell with her fingernail, and popped the peanut into her mouth. Then she put the empty shell back in the bag. Behind us, Blanche sneezed.

"Aren't you going to be hot in that sweater?" I asked Parker.

"Not once we're moving," she answered.

"All right, then," I said. "Looks like we're ready to go."

Simon started his game soon after we left the interstate to coast along one of those leafy two-lane highways that wove through every settlement with a bar and grocery store. Blanche lifted her face into the streaming wind, flying her tongue like a meat-pink flag. Simon folded his arms along the back of my seat and watched the road over my shoulder. "Who's going to have the most sex this weekend? I vote me."

"I vote not you," I snapped back. "She's engaged, I'm involved, and you're meeting up with your ex to trade dog custody." On the steering wheel my hands looked puffy, lined. I needed moisturizer.

Parker shifted in the seat next to me. "I didn't know you had a boyfriend, Dana."

"Girlfriend," Simon said with a smug grin. I glanced over at Parker. Pale face, pale freckles, pale unmoving lips.

"We've been together since August," I said.

"Funny Ivan never mentioned that," Parker said.

"You're not getting married till May," Simon said. "And bachelorette parties are for screwing around."

Parker fidgeted with her sweater, her perfect French-manicured nails skimming up and down the zipper. "No one said this was a bachelorette party," I said. "At least we'll go out to the clubs. All you and Bruce Lee will do is stay indoors and fight."

"His name is Matt," Simon said placidly. "You forget the benefits of consolatory sex. I propose a mutual vow: we'll all keep each other's secrets. I won't tell Ivan or Corey anything that happens this weekend."

"And what do you want from us?"

"Did I say bargain? I meant blackmail leverage." Simon riffed a hand through his carrot hair, composed.

Parker stirred. "I've never cheated on a boyfriend in my life." She crossed her legs, one knee over the other.

"I wish I could say the same," Simon mourned. "Dana?"

"I've only had one serious boyfriend," I said. "If you can call it that."

"You played for the other team?" Simon leaned forward even further, his jaw jutting over my right shoulder. "When? How long?"

"Two years." I kept my hands firmly on the wheel, ten and two o'clock.

"It was while I was at North Florida. Everybody called him Rebel."

"Jewish," Simon guessed.

"Cherokee, seven-eighths."

"And beautiful, I'll bet." Simon sighed. "You little man-eating devil, you." He pretended to snap at my ear. "There's always room for one more beautiful man."

"Not this one," I said.

Rebel had been two years ahead of me in the archaeology program. His name on the school roster was David, his Cherokee name something I couldn't pronounce. The man had many names and no handles. I followed him through four semesters and two summers of field work around the Ocklockonee and its tributaries, staking settlement outlines and sifting through kitchen debris, while he dove the rivers and looked for traces of the Apalachee. In his sleep he held me so tightly that I didn't dare move; I'd touch his scarred face, his scarred knee, and wonder about these stories that he wouldn't tell me. I promised myself I would be the one to leave him.

Then he graduated and went back to the Southwest, the desert acreage and copper arroyos a better backdrop for his complexion. He took the Dana that I knew and left a hostage in her place. I skipped too many classes, switched majors, tended bar, ended up in a series of beds attached to bodies without faces. I'd had girlfriends before him and after, but that man tore through me like lightning. Corey, sweet and organized with her paper planner and address book, doesn't understand how I can have no idea where he is. She sends handmade birthday cards to her ex-girlfriends.

"You've cheated on Corey before," Simon said, and Parker's thin shoulders twitched.

"Only once. And she knows about it." The memory still brought a powdery acid to my mouth, not the indiscretion, but the confession. It sounded so cheap when I told her, New Year's in Indianapolis with the old cronies from Father Thomas Scecina Memorial, everybody drunk with the pulsing lights and hallucinogenic music, Greg's hand up my skirt to the tune of Dana I've always loved you, just you, girl. Desire, such a potent illusion when mixed with alcohol and long distance. In revenge Corey went on two coffee dates and kissed the pert new assistant in the dean's office. Things haven't been the same since. We keep asking each other the same questions twice.

"Are you wearing sunblock?" I quizzed Parker. I couldn't imagine Ivan cheating on anybody. He didn't have the tact.

"SPF 45," Parker said, picking lint off her seat. "Thanks for doing this, Dana."

"I'm not doing anything except down-shifting this car far too often."

"No, really. Your aunt has the perfect dress for me. It's nice of you to bring me along when you visit her, so I can get the fitting out of the way."

Nice. She used the word nice. Unironically. "It's my car," Simon volunteered.

"Your father's car. And he asked me to drive because he's terrified you'll break something."

"It's a nice car," Parker allowed.

"The boys like it." He fluttered his eyelashes at her, and she looked away.

I glanced at her, profile like the Sphinx, saving the complete nose. If she tried to mock Simon, who wore his heart so close to his skin that you could practically see the blood rushing through the red-gold chambers—Simon, who had cried in my arms over Matt with more heartbreak than I had ever seen in anyone, with more bereavement than I had ever shown for Rebel— if she even thought about ridiculing him, she would get a suitcase dropped on her foot, be left alone in a restaurant while I went to the bathroom, promises to Ivan be damned.

"Tell me, Dana," Parker said, watching the ranks of pine woods file past us, "how you and Ivan got to be such good friends."

"You and Ivan are friends?" Simon lifted his glasses. "Dana, I thought you said that Ivan's emotional IQ hit a temperature at which plant life could not survive."

It took me a while to understand Ivan gravitated to me because he thought me safe, a neutral zone, immune. Because I was not small and pretty, because I had Corey, because I did not wear high heels. For a few weeks of sweat-soaked nights I lay awake with visions of a perfectly normal hetero future for me and Ivan: marriage, sex and fighting, babies, divorce when we hit middle-age. I had not foreseen the strange intellectual courtship, the constant attention devoid of even the most passing intimation of lust, the way I would drive him home after dinners or parties or dancing and pretend I didn't want him to ask me in.

I wondered if Parker knew that after the spring semester welcome party Ivan and I had lain on the hood of my car drunk with too much boxed wine and he told me how he'd fought with his father, how his ex was about to be married. The redbirds beat out their staccato call and I said, "I'm bi, you know." Even though I was with Corey and fully perceived her warmth, her goodness, I knew that if he had touched me then everything else would have gully-washed away; I would have risen like the spring floods in the desert, I would have offered all the crumbling pieces of me that Rebel had left behind. But he was silent and I went home and two weeks later he was engaged to Parker, and I was sure that one day I would wake up in my bed with Corey and feel that this woman, this cocoon of safety, this warm nest with its blue ceiling and dim light and peeling old paint all, somehow, belonged to me.

"Ivan and I share the same literary tastes," I told Parker. "I'm the only one in our program who has read everything by Roger Zelazny."

"That's nothing. You should see his comic book collection," Parker said. She turned her face to look out at the yellow-green check of passing meadows and groves, away.

"She has," Simon twittered.

I elbowed his hand off my headrest. "You think Bruce Lee would take you back if he knew what you've been poking around in the last six months?"

"Tell him anything about me," Simon said comfortably, "and I'll out you to your parents." He nudged a CD over the seat. "Play."

I shut my mouth, put the disc in the console, and we listened to "It's Raining Men" until the outskirts of Bay City rose up before us like a glittering desert mirage.

Rebel was the one who told me that this whole area used to live off its clam beds, until the contractors fished the beds dry and paved the streets with mollusk shells. The sport fish migrated out into the bay and the famous Apalachicola clam snapped its way south, leaving the Bay City council to launch a desperately garish claim to have the whitest! the most sparkling! beaches! in the world!! Developers filled in with cement the remains of the fishing settlement while resort hotels and wharf bars reared over the open waiting shell of thousands of square yardage of sand shipped in from the Caribbean each year. Half-alive during the scorching months, battened down with wood and steel during the hurricane season, Bay City lurked in slumberous apathy through the summer until life returned in the late-fall boom of snow birds flurrying toward their winter quarters. Once mid-February spawned the warming trends and the flowers began to bloom, masses and masses of college students surged into the City, throttling its four-lane bridge, clogging the T-shirt shops and tattoo parlors, venting the exhaust of vans and SUVs into the once-quiet air and polluting the pristine beaches with the residual fluids of their favorite vacation activities, sex and drinking and vomiting up their drinks in order to consume further quantities of alcohol before racketing their scooters up and down the main thoroughfare. I avoided spending my spring break on the beaches even when I attended North Florida; I've never been part of a herd.

I had imagined that our hotel, advertised as beach-side, would be a cabana with a breezeway, ranks of potted plants, chairs upon which to relax and view the sunset, where I could run straight out my door in the morning and dive into the water. Ivan found the hotel, since my aunt Nat didn't have room for guests at her cottage. Our fitting was booked for Saturday morning, and Aunt Nat was doing a trade show that night, leaving our evening terrifyingly open.

Ivan, it turned out, had selected a brand-name chain hotel, and our room, third floor (safer! no burglar access, the manager on duty insisted), opened onto the interior hallway. The floor-to-ceiling windows, insulated and triple-sealed, could withstand gale-force winds. Balconies meant higher insurance, the manager explained. Drunk kids falling off them, I supposed, or drunk frat boys climbing up them into rooms, and possibly vaginas, that did not belong to them. I cursed and threw my canvas bag into the closet. Simon smuggled Blanche in his backpack. Parker dialed the air conditioner to an arctic 8.

Changing into my bathing suit I heard the hallway door close, then a short questioning yip from the dog.

"Simon better not have stuck us with the mutt," I called, tying the neck strap of my lime-green one-piece. I cinched the beach towel around my waist and then patted my hips, liking the warm weight of them, round as scallops.

"He said he'd be back. Nice doggy. Nice Blanche."

I stepped out of the bathroom to find Parker sitting with one foot propped on the table, dragging a dry razor over her extended legs. Blanche nudged at the door with a bristled muzzle and whined.

Parker's body in her bathing suit was a study in angles, the flat plane of her nape curtained by briskly short black hair, the bones curving bravely beneath her skin, the scoop of her collarbone, the knobs of her pelvis jutting out like a gate. The string of her bikini top—pink, with small black polka-dots—clutched a neck slender as a flower stem. The vertebrae in her spinal cord lined up like a row of sand dollars. Without thinking I felt my hands go to my own convex belly. Wherever Parker had angles, I had curves.

I moved to the window to survey the beach. Tan bodies dotted the white sand like figures on an ancient wall carving. In the reflected room I watched the razor cruise up Parker's shin, jag suddenly over her knee. A thin red line squeezed out and she yelped.

"Put your finger on it and it will stop in a minute."

"Ew." Her tiny princess nose wrinkled at me, a five-year-old looking at a plate of beets. "Don't you have a Band-aid?"

"Oh, mother of God." It was just a baby cut, on the little bump of her knee bone. I licked my finger and pressed it over the tiny pore of red. Parker inhaled horrifically.

"Give it ten seconds and it will clot," I instructed.

Helpless, panting sounds escaped her, Blanche-like. "What's the matter? Germs? You bleed once a month, in case you hadn't noticed."

"I don't." Parker's voice squeaked like a door hinge. "I haven't had my period since I was in eighth grade."

Her skin was cool and smooth as a pad of chilled butter. How thin her tissues must be on the inside, just enough to hold her together, a little protein and a lot of stubborn. This was the body Ivan wanted to touch every inch of, the pale almost-invisible freckles and the raised mole-hill freckles, the body he knew inside and out. Into the space between us swelled the curves of my own generous body, the ballast of my bottom, my breasts like gourds, the swell of my stomach that Ivan never would, had not ever wanted to lay his hands upon or lie next to.

"Maybe if you stopped starving yourself and ate something?" I lifted my finger, peeked, squished the pad back against her skin. "It won't clot if you're anemic."

"There are such things as vitamins," Parker said. The small button of crushed crimson on the knob of her knee looked innocently at me; I licked a different finger and scrubbed at the button till it vanished into a tiny slit, demurely pursed.

"I can't believe you just did that."

I tossed the sunblock at her and headed back to the bathroom, imagining if Ivan ever cut himself shaving, the scene that would ensue: rushes for the first aid kit, the Betadine and gauze, the panic of two people as sterile and hyper-clean as laboratory specimens. I refused to understand how a person, a human being, could not like her own messy body with all its extraordinary fluids and functions. Whole weekends passed where Corey and I neglected even to shower, spent the hours of daylight rolling around in the bed of our combined sweat, slick as dolphins, naked as geese. She'd walk to the bathroom and kick clothes out of her way, her legs shimmering like Aphrodite of the sea, shouting "Naked! Nobody wears clothes here!" I'd whistle at her when she bent over to pick up a magazine, grabbing for the soft roll around her middle.

Rebel approached sex with silent intensity, though he was a biter, anywhere he could reach. He liked to inspect me in the morning for marks he'd made the night before, satisfied that his anger had burned its way onto my skin. I shivered slightly as I rubbed sunblock into my legs. Ivan probably showered before and after sex. Maybe during. Not that I would know.

A sky peppered with parasailers and water cloudy with bodies met us as Parker and I flip-flopped our way through the glazed sand. Half a foot taller than her, I felt like a Valkyrie, armed with beach towel instead of spear. Beside me Parker drew male gazes like a compass needling to north. She kept her chin up. The dark glasses hugged her eyes. I've always had this figure, solid. Rebel called me an armful. Corey scorns girls with delicate bodies, calls them choir girls. She would have called Parker flat, or fleshless, but in reality she was perfectly proportioned, a miniature piece of sculpture, a Cloisonné vase. I stabbed our beach umbrella into an unoccupied triangle of sand and Parker set up a canvas chair. I sipped a San Pellegrino and she opened a Pepsi. Frisbees whizzed over our heads.

This was where Corey and I would start gossiping about the people around us. Parker pulled out a copy of the latest Danielle Steel. She was, I observed, one of those people who kept her place by dog-earing pages. I, in anticipation of talking and swimming and perhaps joining in a game of volleyball, had brought nothing to read.

"Well," I said, raising my bottle, "happy bachelorette party to us."

After about a millennium of silence, Simon picked his way over, puckering his lips prima-donna style, lacking one small fuzzy dog but escorting a smooth male specimen with muscles that had been built over thousands of patient hours in the gym, and a jaw that bent space and time around it.

"Hello, bachelorettes!" Simon boomed. He wore a one-piece man's bathing suit, orange with black stripes, the kind that went out of style circa 1900. Bruce Lee sported spandex trunks that hugged every dip and dimple.

"This is Matt," Simon informed us, smirking. Matt nodded briefly so as not to dislodge the sunglasses balanced on his gleaming black hair. Simon pushed my legs off the blanket and sat down, swilling my Pellegrino. Parker pulled her paperback closer to her face. Matt stepped away and struck a Qigong posture.

"Are you," I began, watching him, and then said, "Never mind."

"You bet I am." Simon practically smacked his lips. "Dana, you don't know what you're missing."

Parker unrolled onto her blanket, face up, ignoring the ancient Chinese meditations and the louder, buzzing Frisbees of the group of boys still trying to get her attention. She curled her toes into the sand, pushed up her glasses, closed her eyes. I thought of how Corey's lips had tasted like raspberry popsicle as she kissed me goodbye, firmly, a bit wildly, and said, "No cheating!"

"I've had that. I'm not missing anything," I said, pushing all thoughts of Rebel away. It had been years. The man didn't get this much of me. He didn't still get to hurt.

Simon turned to Parker. "Tell us about Ivan the Viking. Does he have the stamina to match his physique?"

Parker gave Simon what could only be a coy smile and lay there, cool as a clam nestled on her blanket. "Ivan's a minute-man," she said, meeting his dare. "But he's very open to suggestion."

Simon hooted. "Selfish lover?" I guessed, recalling how Ivan had never so much as brushed an elbow against me, even when I was holding his plate of cheese.

Parker chuckled. The sound was thick and deep, not at all the kind of laugh I expected from her. "It's not his fault," she said to Simon. "I'm an excellent faker."

"Me too," Simon said.

"That's why I like girls," I said, oiling mango-scented glycerin into my palm and striping it over my calves. "Girls notice these things." The warm firm sand made me miss Corey. The two of us were like porn directors shouting out suggestions for a scene. "Harder! Try that! There!" We used the Olympic scale before, during, and after. We laughed frequently.

"I've never been attracted to a woman," Parker murmured. Her tiny palm, chalk-white, lay on the sand between us.

"Me neither," Simon agreed, leaning back on his arms and looking lustfully at his companion. I snapped shut the sunblock tube and kept my legs pulled up to hide my stomach. Matt, ignoring our vanities, folded himself into Crane Pose and gazed nobly out to sea.

Simon and Matt strolled off arm in arm sometime later, dissolving into the dusk. Parker and I were enveloped by the Frisbee players, most of whom crowded around her; one of them, Lucky, distinctive by the backwards slant of his baseball cap, regarded me.

"You're in our hotel," he said. "I saw you chewing the manager's ass." His eyes glowed. So did his skin, smooth and tanned and sun-oiled. Sand splashed up his legs and dotted his baggy swim trunks. His hair, much the same color, stuck out shaggily beneath the cap. His teeth were very even and too white. He reminded me of my cousin Barry, a real Florida boy, born and bred in Pensacola, oozing sex and swagger.

"Right," I said. "Ass chewing is one of my particular talents."

"Hey, come on. Hang out with us." Lucky gave me a wicked grin. "You can show me what your other talents are."

Oh, this modern culture, I thought; only gay boys longed for romance. Straight ones just wanted to hit it and get out. I swung the beach bag onto my shoulder, clipping the ribs of the nearest frat boy. He jumped back, breaking the circle. I put my hand over the square of Parker's elbow. "My girlfriend wouldn't like that," I said sweetly, "and neither would her fiancé. See you later, boys."

Parker didn't feel like going out, so we got fried food and slushies at a roadside stand and took them back to the room. Simon had removed his luggage. Blanche had peed on one of the beds.

"Call housekeeping," Parker said, showing her five-year-old princess nose again. "We can't sleep here with that smell."

"If housekeeping finds us with Simon's dog, we're out of a place to

40

sleep tonight," I informed her. "This whole city is completely booked this time of year, and my Aunt Nat, sweet as she is, doesn't have the room." Parker wandered restlessly, pinching at her bathing suit, while I stripped the covers, threw them into the bathtub, and turned on the water. Blanche squinted at me with eyes like black diamonds, muzzle curved into a stupid smile.

We wasted little of our evening in conversation. Parker coaxed Blanche to her with bits of chicken wing while we watched old movies on AMC. The sun set outside our window in sprawling glory, casting peacock streaks of rose and copper and bronze across the sky. I cracked open the first bottle of pink champagne I had brought, the cheapest available, and handed Parker a Styrofoam cup. We never laughed at the same places of the movie.

When Ivan called, she took her cell phone out into the hallway for about fifteen minutes. She returned to tell me, "Ivan says hi."

"How nice of him," I said. "Tell him I say hi back."

Somewhere into the second bottle of champagne, Parker pulled on her sweatpants and crawled into the remaining bed. I drew the comforter and an extra pillow onto the floor and tucked the cool bottle next to me, seeing the late night movie through to its credits and thinking of Corey, on retreat with the LGTBSA alliance, giggling and playing truth or dare. I turned off the light and watched the moon slant blue shadows into the room. Parker didn't snore but Blanche did, snuffling into her crossed paws, body drawn into a spotted half-shell on the slope of sheet next to Parker's head. I imagined the sort of dares Corey would get: flashing, streaking, body paint, striptease. She'd have a ball until she challenged them back and said, truth. And they, inquisitive bitches, would only have one question: Are you going to stay with Dana or not?

My aunt Nat's bridal shop stood tucked between a fish fry place and a tourist mini-mart selling T-shirts, surfboards, and rack after rack of bathing suits and sunglasses. I tried prepping Parker to meet my aunt, but apparently chatting on the phone over bust measurements and train lengths had already turned them into old friends. Nat greeted us with impartial enthusiasm, giving us each a kiss on the cheek. Her lips felt like worn cotton, soft and thin. The mirrored fitting room with its violet trim and pots of ferns was wide and cozy, with reed chimes dangling in the open window. It occurred to me, seeing them face to face, that Parker and my aunt resembled each other: small and sly and slender, knowing more than they let on.

"Your mother thought you'd be earlier," Nat murmured, holding my hand and looking me over. She smelled of orange peel and rosemary.

"We had to take the dog for a walk first." I'd packed my one summer dress and wore it in deference, knowing Nat liked to see women gowned. Her coiffed white hair showed a pink tinge and the yards of beads around her neck clacked like an abacus when she moved. My mother was ten years younger and had always been insulted by her older half-sister, this expression showing as early as the baby picture that Nat kept on her desk.

"I hope you won't mind if we catch up for a while, dear," Nat said to Parker, producing a plate of lemon cookies and a pitcher of sparkling water. "Dana, I thought you would bring your girlfriend to meet me?"

"Who told you I have a girlfriend?" I choked on cookie, white sugar grating down my throat. Parker sat on the other side of the couch, knees and hands pressed together.

"Your cousin Barry? My son? Some children communicate with their parents." Nat handed me a napkin and brushed away the crumbs on the front of my dress.

"You try telling her," I gasped, reaching for my glass of water. "You just try."

"Oh, I know my sister," Aunt Nat misted. She tipped her chin at Parker. "When our father died, I talked to a therapist, but my sister—she got born again." She picked another picture off her desk. Within a frame of rose-laden vines, Nat, full-faced and gleaming, clung to the arm of her first husband; my mother, foxy and dark, scowled from the flush of lace choking her bridesmaid's dress, a flower askew in her hair.

"Can you imagine?" Aunt Nat said. "People die every day. But Trish took it personally."

"She spends her spare time looking through bridal magazines," I said to Parker. "I think she might actually murder me when she finds out I'm not going to fulfill her dream. It would be like a TV movie. I would ruin her entire life."

Aunt Nat sniffed. "We have two of them on the Cordova side. That's my dead husband's family, may he rest in peace," she said for Parker's sake. "Your uncle Huey is gay, and Stephanie, she's your second cousin, she just came out."

"Somehow I don't think that will help me with Patricia."

She sniffed again, her little ski-slope nose twitching at the end. "Now you, dear." She turned to Parker with a flattering smile. "Tell me everything about your husband-to-be: when you met, how he proposed, everything."

I turned to Parker expectantly. This I wanted to hear. Ivan told me nothing of the details: if they fought, if sometimes he found her just a little bit unformed. What Parker did with herself the nights he called me wanting to go out for a drink. He only ever talked about books or math, his duplicitous ex, how he and his father had stopped speaking. I wondered sometimes if I wanted Ivan because I still wanted to reach Rebel, to become the person it would have been impossible for him to leave. Or maybe there was just something I was looking to finish, so I could be the one who packed up my heart and my belongings and walked away into the sticky night.

"Ours is a really boring story, actually," Parker said. Tiny indentations appeared at the corners of her lips. "The education department came to the interior design program when they wanted to redesign their student lounge. So I went over there one day with some fabric swatches, and there he was." She sat with her hands folded neatly over her knees, the way I knew my mother always wished I would sit.

Nat put a hand to her tailored pink jacket, pressing her heart. "So sweet," said my aunt, who had divorced two husbands after the first died. "Wait a moment, will you, dears?"

The moment she stepped out of the room, Parker and I turned to each other.

"I'm sorry if—" I started to say, but Parker held up her hand.

"She's so lovely," she said. "I'm so glad I got to meet her, Dana."

I realized that hand gesture was exactly what my aunt would do.

Nat promenaded back into the room like the grail maiden, holding something filmy and trailing. "I wanted this for you, Dana, but . . ."

"Save it for Barry," I said, stuffing another cookie into my mouth. "Barry's wife."

"Barry won't get married either. He's too sophisticated for that. My line will die out. But you, dear," she said, placing the veil on Parker's head.

"It's beautiful." Parker regarded the accessory with the reverential awe other people might accord the artifacts of a lost civilization. She and Nat were nearly the same height, had the same cupped, robin-like head. The veil frothed around Parker's face like sea mist, softening her sharp features, giving her the look of a woman well-loved. Even her freckles seemed subdued.

I had to zip Parker into her princess gown, strapless and plunging, a Cinderella concoction of lace and seed pearls and satin rustling like the feathers of terns, draped with enough tulle to supply three different fishing boats with net and sail. Her bared shoulders cut the air like blades. She agonized over the exact shade of white to dye her shoes: Ivory? Pearl? Wistful snow? Aunt Nat took up her pincushion and circled like a diving rod, dipping back and forth. Through subtle questioning and advice she managed to arrange every detail of Parker's ceremony, from the jewelry to be worn by her bridesmaids—sorority sisters who had all graduated and found work—and the flower arrangements—sprays of white lilies—to the type of champagne to serve at the reception and what to say discreetly to keep the groomsmen from drinking too much. I didn't know who to admire more: my aunt, who needled people without their noticing, or Parker, who could turn to glass in an instant and allow everything to slip off her like water.

It needed only incense and chanting to make the moment complete. What more primal ceremony could there be among women than the ritual adornment before offering one of their kind for mating with the opposite of the species? But there must have always been the women like me, women who didn't want a man tracking mud and leaves into her cave. There must have been hands that met over the cookpot, gazes that lingered, shoulders that brushed while the women were gathering berries and weaving mats and doing all the others thousand things that ensured the life and comfort of the clan. Sappho sang of the most exquisite, passionate love while the male poets orated about warfare and heroics. What happened to the women like me, who didn't go to protectors, who were moved by fullness and vigor and litheness and beauty no matter what form it came in? Had there ever been a place, a ritual, a way of being for us?

In the mirror the pristine lace corona floated about Parker's head like a delicious, magical secret. Nat had not asked me if I wanted the veil.

I ejected myself onto the sidewalk, into the burning sun, and asked for a cigarette from the back of a male head with the baseball cap facing me.

"Shut up! I know you!" It was, mother of all curses, Lucky. The rest of the dumb squad was desecrating the T-shirt shop. He grinned at me as I leaned in to let him light my cigarette and I saw how smooth the skin of his face was, how fine the hairs, like the bristles of tiny anemones. He caught me staring at his lips and brought his face closer and I held still, feeling his lips touch mine briefly, a warm and fluttering softness.

"I wasn't kidding about my girlfriend," I said, flicking ash onto the pavement, right next to his sandaled feet.

"Not the one in there." He pointed with his chin at the bridal shop, somewhere within it a gown floating on ten yards of satin, and somewhere within that, Parker's tiny voice and wide eyes. Scared. As she looked at herself in the three-way mirror, skin beneath the freckles one-half shade darker than the dress, she'd looked afraid that it might suddenly eat her. Swallow her and leave nothing behind, not even bones to pick the teeth with.

"No. Not her." My voice wisped with smoke.

"Good." He smiled, briefly, his lips precise and perfectly proportioned. "Come to Harpoon Harry's."

"No."

"I'll show you where I saw the dolphins."

No means no, I wanted to say, just to be mean. I couldn't sleep with him and pretend Rebel could be put to rest, or this strange pull toward Ivan could be forgotten, or Corey could be wiped away like a smudge on a slide. He reminded me in that moment of Greg from Father Scecina's; they shared a certain flare of cheekbone, a delicacy of hand. I felt a hollowness in my chest from too many memories, the old loves like catacombs, some dusty and almost forgotten, some revisited so often they became polished as shrines.

"I'm really not your type." I said it casually, wrist tucked under my elbow, cigarette waving beneath his nose.

"Who cares." He reached out and with his fingertip touched my neck below my right ear. One touch, his hand soft like seawater. How often the surfaces of people slide past one another, eddied in their own currents. How rarely those surfaces touch.

"Come out tonight," he said again. "It's all cool." He rolled his shoulders and pulled off the cap and smoothed his hair and put the cap on again, backwards, as he walked away.

"I'm done." Parker stood framed in another doorway, as she seemed fated to be: always standing with someone looking at her, demanding something. Standing as though she weren't sure where to place herself in the room, like a stool or a floor lamp.

"Sorry." I mashed out the cigarette and placed it on the rim of the nearest trash can. "I couldn't breathe in there. Gilt makes me nervous."

"Wasn't that one of the guys from the beach?"

"Free shots if we go to Harpoon Harry's tonight." Where the hell was Simon? It was at least eighteen hours until we were scheduled to leave.

I went back inside to say goodbye to Nat and she held me close for a long moment, then cupped my cheek. "Don't forget to exfoliate, dear. Keeps the skin young."

"I love you too, Aunt Nat." I kissed the corner of her mouth. She waved at us out of her window as we walked past, the curtains flushing her face a powdery pink. I knew the second we were out of sight she would call my mother.

"Let's do something crazy," Parker said as we walked back to the hotel. She clutched the boxed veil that Nat had given her.

"How crazy?" I said.

"Something I can do now that I'll never do when I'm married."

So we went parasailing. That says an awful lot about Ivan, if you think about it. Parker, too.

Blanche was still in the room when we returned, snug behind the Do Not Disturb sign. We put on tight clothing and went to Harpoon Harry's and, as I predicted, drank for free all night. The frat boys converged on Parker, ringing her with their inflated chests, but Lucky peeled me away, suggesting a walk on the beach. He held my hand at the small of his back as he pushed a way for us down the stairs, and I decided I would let him touch me.

He was more bashful than I expected, a practiced kisser but gentle, almost shy. After I pulled off my dress and threw it down he picked it up, shook out the sand, and folded it neatly atop his own shorts and T-shirt. We stood waist-deep in a warm gulf that touched foreign lands hundreds of miles away, with so much ancient and unfathomable in between. His skin grew smoother with a layer of sea-salt, and I liked the cool slide of his tongue. But neither of us had a condom tucked anywhere, and this was the conversation we were having when Simon came to the edge of the water and bellowed my name, dredging up my obligations to Parker.

"You babysit Parker a mother-loving minute!" I bellowed back at him.

He budged not, hands at his hips, silk shirt unbuttoned most of the way down his chest. "I'm not giving you one of my condoms, I'm using all of them tonight. Fun's over, boys and girls. Now you see the beauty of our system," he added to me as I trudged back to shore. The night air felt warm and sharp and empty. I swiped up my dress.

Back at the bar I found Parker with one hand clamped over the top of her Solo cup, eyes glassy as a doll's, her backless shirt smeared with sweat, none of it hers. I planted myself next to her and tried to intercept the groping hands, not for Ivan's sake but for her, so small and clad in acrylics. The incessant thump of the bass line started a reverb in my chest. Before long the inevitable happened and the dumb squad proclaimed we had to kiss before they'd buy us another round. "Kiss! Kiss!" they chanted, waving red plastic glasses sloshing with beer, trumpeting the age-old assumption of the male that the world must bend itself to his fantasies. Parker reached a butterfly hand behind my neck and kissed me. She closed her eyes furiously and her teeth banged against mine, her lips cool, her breath amaretto, her hand on the back of my neck as feathery as a palm frond.

Shortly after, she threw up all over the both of us and the circle of foaming red beer cups retreated. In our room, while Blanche sat on the unmade bed and pawed at the covers, I stripped off my clothes and then Parker's, turned on the shower, and propped her under it, holding her up with one arm. I half-pulled the curtain in an attempt at modesty, remembering how she hadn't let either me or Aunt Nat see her white underpants.

"You smell like vomit," she said, her voice muffled by spray.

"So do you. Can I let go or are you going to fall over?"

She pulled back the shower curtain, baring herself at me. "I might fall," she said. "I might pass out and drown."

I stared at her face, beaded with water. Her mascara left half-moon shadows under her eyes and her lips puffed like fresh sashimi. I knew even then that her face would stay with me: like the first night I woke up smothered in Rebel's arms and knew he was going to break me, or the night Ivan and I sat atop my car and I felt myself splintering again, I knew some fragment of me would be stuck eternally in this moment, trapped by her huge eyes, by one more wounded animal using my dense, strong body as a shield. Her tiny pale hand closed around my suntanned wrist and pulled.

"I don't seduce drunk women," I warned her.

"I do," she said, her face fierce and iridescent.

Parker had what surgeons call a virgin abdomen, a smooth stretch of skin unblemished with scars, a flat land, unawakened. Her hair still smelled of the apple shampoo she'd used that morning and she tasted like mouthwash and the chlorine pooling beneath our feet. Even under the warm spray her skin was cool, and I could feel beneath it the tendons, the layers of veins. She was no texture but smooth, like a shellfish, her bones hard and pearled and curving, the flesh inside slick and salty and cool. I expected she would lose her courage as she sobered up, but I underestimated her determination. She didn't speak, so I didn't either, not even when her nails sank like stinging jellyfish into my skin and she shook so hard I thought she was going to come apart in my hands. I was careful. You don't survive a man like Rebel and not learn how to be careful.

She still cried, after. She turned her face into the stream of cooling water and I stepped out and left the last fresh towel for her.

Simon woke us the next morning. He looked terrible, unwashed and rumpled. The hard white lines around his mouth stretched all the way to his eyes. He didn't even smirk when he saw Parker and me lying separately on the bed, backs facing each other. He carried a black leather bag that I hadn't seen before. Matt had given back the last of his things.

I touched his cheek as he sat at the table, forehead in his hand. "Eyelash," I said, stretching out my finger. "Make a wish."

"Not now, Dana." He pushed my hand away. "Tell me about *your* evening."

"I can't," I said, so we ate in silence the pancakes and eggs and bacon that room service delivered. On the bed, Blanche licked herself with noisy effort.

Parker finally emerged from the bathroom and I watched her, looking for what I don't know, some new softness perhaps, some indication that she didn't need to hold herself so tightly anymore. She was in black again, slim as a needle, and she avoided both of us as she picked up her bag and slung it crosswise over her chest. She tucked the pad of hotel stationery and the logoed pen into her purse and waited by the door until Simon and Blanche and I were ready to leave.

We drove back to Valdosta in a silence broken only by Parker's request to stop at the same orange roadside tourist trap so she could buy boiled peanuts for Ivan. I said nothing about alligator heads. Instead I followed Simon to the edge of the pines and watched him take off Blanche's lead. She sniffed at an old trash can for a long time, poking and circling. Then she saw a bird and her ears shot straight up, her tail raised like a flag, and she took off with silent fury. Simon dropped the lead into the trash can.

"Parker's going to wonder where the dog went," I said. I felt sick.

"I want everyone to see," Simon said, blinking quickly. "I want everyone to know what a bastard he is."

But Parker didn't remark on the absence of Blanche. Ivan came down the stairs to meet us as I turned into their parking lot. He was bare-chested in the heat, wearing flip-flops. Rebel had been that beautiful when he walked out of the river, neoprene outlining every muscle of his body, an old god rising from the water.

"Thanks for doing this, Dana," Ivan said. He leaned down to kiss Parker as she went to stand beside him, a black outline in the heat. It was a screen kiss, the lips meeting and clinging briefly, her dark hair falling away from her chin. Then they both turned and he put his hand on her back and they ascended the stairs, up and up, into the apartment that held their life together, shutting the smug blue door.

I took Simon to his father's house and we sat in our seats for a long time, even after I handed him the keys.

"Miracle question," he said. "You wake up tomorrow and everything's better. What changed?"

"Me?" I said, watching the orange-rimmed sunglasses.

He shook his head. "You're right."

Corey cried when I told her. She picked up a tube of paint and threw it against the wall, where it squirted a crimson vein.

"Why couldn't it be the guy?" she cried. "Why couldn't you just let the guy fuck you?"

I looked at the sluice of paint and thought, for once I had made a swift clean break that would bleed freely and heal right. It was a start.

We'd gone parasailing in a double harness; Parker's idea of crazy did not include alone. Two boys brown as chicory roots strapped us in and the boat shot into the bay, hoisting us into the air while the wind pricked open every pore of our bodies. We'd reached maximum height when Parker said, "I'm going to marry a man who can't tell when I fake an orgasm."

I figured this was Parker's version of bachelorette truth or dare, so I said, "I still haven't told my mother I'm bi."

We could see the waves, thousands of little commas smattered across the water, all headed out to sea. The coral and forest greens of the old clam beds, an ancient and lost civilization, shone through the bluest and purest of blue.

Parker turned to face me. Her cheek looked small and curved as a seashell. "I hated you when I met you. I thought Ivan was in love with you. But he said you were hung up on someone else."

I watched the horizon, its single dimension. "I had a crush on him for a while," I said.

We could see the gleam of bumper-to-bumper steel on the frontage road. The hotels up and down the beach sat like tiny square and regular ant hills, busy insect life issuing forth at every second.

"But you want him," I said.

She kept quiet a long time, her mouth a small downward curve, her knees and elbows angled like the most precise origami.

"I think I feel what I need to feel," she said, not looking at me.

I wondered if Corey would send me a birthday card.

We looked at the sky. It went on forever. Other parasailers drifted by us, waving; we had joined the club. When the same sun-brown boys pulled us in and released us from the harness, Parker bent and plucked something from the sand. It was a tiny double-valve shell, each wing as small as the nail of her pinky finger. She snapped it apart and handed one of the shells to me.

"Your souvenir," she said. "Of our first and last time parasailing."

I was glad to think that the next time Nat's wedding veil paraded down the aisle, Parker would be wearing it. I almost wished I would be there.

Corey thought I wanted to trick Ivan, so every time he touched Parker, he was touching me. But it was Parker I wanted to mark. To give her a memory that would linger, half-forgotten, no matter who else skimmed the surface of her, never knowing those impossible depths. Wherever I ended up later, whatever happened and whomever I chose, I had left one grain of myself with her that would be protected, growing hard and pearled and cushioned at the heart of her, my fingerprint on the jewel at her core.

SMOKE INHALATION

You go to the bar because he wants you to; he always wants to go to the bar, it's one of the few places he can smoke and he knows you dislike it but he smokes anyway, heavily, malevolently, lighting the next Marlboro with the one already clamped between his teeth, while the exhaled smoke curls back toward his mouth, towards those lips that for a while you thought of as belonging to you. His hands are shaking again. This is the bar where you drank whiskey sours and he explained quantum physics using cocktail napkins. When the high has him, the buzz over the scalp between the hair and skin, he will be able to tell you what you expect you are here to hear from him, and you suck in your own air, wishing for smoke-free air, toxin-pure air, air to fill your ribs, to tuck in between the beating parts of you, brace you against the incision.

That first night, his knee touched yours under the table. You shared a copulatory gaze. The thoughts, he said, are always chewing at his brain, little animals always chewing, and you thought of mice in the pantry, sharp teeth worrying the paper towels or the perishables, but from the back where you can't see it, don't know until you pick up a bag of rice and it empties itself on the kitchen floor, tiny grains spewing all over the linoleum with the clatter of pennies, a hard white storm.

The smoke stings the linings of your mouth, the inside of your nose, the tissue-thin lids of your eyes. You can taste it at the back of your throat, bitter and dry, like chewing on burlap, like the taste of his mouth on nights like this when he used to come home and kiss you, falling into bed three-parts drunk and two-parts giddy, and what would this conversation look like in the hard light of morning? Perhaps both your complexions fare better by lamp light. He says it's not just you it's everything, and you've begun to see through the carousel horses to the machinery hidden in the heart of it, the truth behind the mirrors: it's not about you. Or, more correctly: Not. You. At all. The rim of the table is sticky with popcorn butter and alcohol and the sweat of so many women who have sat here just as you are, wishing for a knight, wishing for a full night of sleep, wondering if they went to the rows and rows of bottles behind the bar and began to break them one by one, brittle and gleaming, would the liquid wash away or would it linger on the floor, hardening into a crystal pool.

The air here is hazy with smoke, a vulgar, smudgy haze, dirty places, these bars, dark with desperation, the low wooden beams of the ceiling absorbing dust, the dim lights leering behind painted canopies, the light pricking on those rows and rows of bottles. Your beer sits before you, sweating, the both of you, the beer in its logoed glass, you in your lambswool-angora sweater, itching at your throat like the burn of a cigarette (it will smell like smoke for a long time coming, no matter how many times you dry clean) and it will take more than ashtrays and empty glasses to span the few inches of bar table that gape like a chasm, bottomless, empty. Someone else has cut his hair.

Did you say you loved him once? Perhaps you used the word with friends, a word not to be bandied about or made common, a word as private as his voice on the phone surprising you at the office, "Hello, beautiful." You said he had a mischievous smile. You loved, yes, the weight of him when he slept in your arms, when you pressed your lips to the baby-soft skin beneath his ear, when he clutched you as he woke and for the first second didn't know where he was.

And what would that skin feel like now, where has the softness gone? There is no magic here in this boisterous music and odiferous smoke. Love has whisked itself away to a ceiling beam, weighted with dust. Love sealed itself back into its peapod each time the phone did not ring. Love opened the window and slipped out like a thief, taking all the words with it, "hello beautiful" echoing down the street just a stream of lost syllables, their own utopia, a no-place of words, a lost echo. If he reached for you now your hand would slide away, keeping that precise distance, like the opposite ends of a magnet. Or: you would cling like saran wrap. The poles have switched themselves around now: north, south, love, silence. Scratch your neck. Scratch, scratch.

He finishes his drink and launches into his script you've anticipated, and oh dear these are the trite words, the ridiculous words: they are already abashed at themselves. He holds a cigarette the way Humphrey Bogart does, wanting to be tall and debonair, but he is too short and his teeth gnash the filter nervously. In his mind this is a daring episode of his life, a dramatic reveal, yet these are not the new and improved words, this is the rather awkward original problem, the problem of choices, of multiplicity and triplicity or simple duplicity; you still do not understand quantum physics, that bit about the particle being in several places at once, yet there is another woman where you are supposed to be, another woman who has been stealing down his hallway late at night falling off her high heels, there is something he didn't intend to happen happening (ha! intention, that twisted snake), and as he must have rehearsed this in the mirror beforehand, with various tilts of the head, the words have already been rubbed-down, become stale, emerging as flat as your beer. Of course, he didn't know how to tell you. But you are feeling helpful at the moment, so you say to him, helpfully, as you stand, grabbing your jacket: You just say it. Just. Like. That.

You make a wonderful exit, not common or vulgar at all but oh, so elegant, the sharp Katherine Hepburn grace as you sweep out of the room, tripping a little at the top of the stairs but by then no one is watching you. Slam your car door emphatically. You smell like stale smoke and mockery, like old jokes. The radio, with a complete lack of irony, sings of rejection and lost loves. Oh, heartbreak! Oh, sarcasm. Your eyes water once, after you sneeze. Here is what he has left you with: allergies. The square roofs of buildings telegraph past your window like a code you don't know how to read. The street lights squat on their overhead wires: Yellow. Red. Red still.

And what has you taken from you, really? Nothing, not your devotion, neither your heart nor any other organ (unless you count a percentage of reduced lung capacity), some time maybe but little else has he wanted from you; he has left you like dust under the couch, spilled sugar on the floor, sticky and clingy and over-stepped as another woman, giggling tipsily, careens down the hallway into his arms. The lines of the city all point somewhere else. You are nothing but a warm bed he slept in once, wishing the window were open.

Slam out of your car in your own driveway, as angry as you like, and then you will finally notice them, lowering themselves out of the sky: the stars, swaths of them. When you were young you would have said they shone from their bed of black velvet like diamonds—back then you had no irony, either—and diamonds at this age are dangerous things but here you have it, a woman standing alone in a shower of tiny lights.

How pure that distance, how clean the spaces between. Like it or not, there will be no more stumbling down hallways for you. The cigarette smoke rises into the atmosphere. Imagine it venting like steam from a hot spring, scouring your lungs, departing your skin, removing itself from the cells and crevices of your body. The night air scrubs away all the traces. The stars do not wink, after all. They are a bit stern, drawing out the shadow of the ridiculous. They've seen all. This. Before.

Spread your arms wide and you can almost feel them, just beyond the reach of your fingertips. They could lift you up and carry you away. Spin a little, the way you did when you were a girl, when you had your projects to do and the woods to explore (so serious you were about all this!) and your stuffed animals led secret fantasy lives almost as active as yours. There is so much to shake off here, to cast from you like smoke. Your chest will be clear soon. So will your head. All you need to fill you is this light.

UNSAID

It starts out as a burn across her forearm, a small thing in itself, about two inches long. When I notice she pulls her hand back, hiding it beneath the café table.

"Oh, it's nothing. I was taking a pan of brownies out of the oven. You know what I klutz I am."

She has a laugh that sounds false even when it's not. If I heard that laugh in a movie theater, not knowing her, I would think her the one who didn't get the joke but chuckled because everyone else did.

Angeline has never been clumsy and I have known her for a long time. In elementary school she was the delicate girl who spent recess in the art room and never spoke in class, while I was the ragged-haired tomboy outrunning the boys on the soccer field. In middle school she sang in the choir while I played volleyball and swam. But in seventh grade we were seated side by side in the misery of Mr. Berg's earth science class and yoked together for all the partner projects, and now we have been friends for more than half our lives. I'm compact and broad-shouldered, built like a bulldog, of peasant stock. Angeline walks like a dancer, slender back straight, as though balancing something on her head.

"Look, it's going to snow this weekend," she says to change the subject.

"It never snows in south Georgia."

"It says here! Our trusty weatherman. I'll have to cover my azaleas." She waves the newsprint at me.

"I don't think your plants are in danger." I move my coffee mug to the center of the table so I don't spill. I'm the clumsy one, not her.

"Remember the last time it snowed? Everything closed down. Businesses. School. My stepdad put chains on his tires. You don't remember? Atlanta had two inches."

I remember. It was the winter we were fourteen. I made my dad drive me through the slippery streets to Angeline's house for a sleepover. We played truth or dare and I dared her to run around the outside of her house barefoot and in her pajamas. The freezing rain left a hard, glossy icing that broke into tiny sharp crystals when she stepped on it. I waited on the back porch, rubbing my arms and shivering, and when she came running up I saw the dark red stain in every other footprint, a perfect round circle, like a drop of raspberry Kool-Aid. She cut her heel on the stump of her mother's rosebush and didn't feel it. I sopped the blood with a dishtowel and then cleaned out the cut with the first aid skills I learned at Girl Scout camp. She laughed about it, that fake-sounding, canned laughter. I tried to think, at the time, what those crimson stains in the snow meant. Why they had been so frightening.

Tuesdays are our best friend days. I don't have to be at the store and she doesn't have any calls. She works for the foster care system, organizing homes, educating parents, rescuing bleeding and abused and abandoned children. She can take down a man three times her size if she thinks he's hurting a baby. Yet there is that burn standing out on her forearm, a fat pink caterpillar, swollen and brooding. Of course I blame Ryan. If she had taken the pan out of the oven and set it to cool, and say he pushed her, and she grabbed the kitchen counter to keep from falling . . . Maybe it was only an embrace. Maybe it was only an accident.

I read her the funnies to make her laugh and she twirls her hair, those long dark tresses with a natural wave. Her sweater falls over her forearm, hiding the caterpillar. It's still his fault; she was making the brownies for him. She doesn't like sweets. Ryan might not know this, but I do.

He comes into my store that Saturday, looking for plywood. He's finally going to finish the basement. I told Angeline I could do it myself. We hash over wiring code, drop ceilings, what she wants for the floor. People look at us like we're a couple as we walk through the store. The night we met him, at the fast food place after basketball practice, he slid into the booth next to me and pressed his thigh against mine. I noticed his shoulders, his forearms, his hands. The next day he called me asking for Angeline's number. He said she had beautiful eyes.

He's not Angeline's type, yet there he was showing up at dance recitals, prom, graduation. Every time she broke up with him he begged for my help getting her back. I wonder now why I gave it. He talks about her softness, her grace, her quiet voice. I, in my steel-toed boots and bright orange tool apron, am not even a woman to him. These broad hips, like shoulders, can bear many things.

"We'll have a good and proper party once the place is done, Sal," he tells me at the register. "There'll be a regular romp room."

"Just be careful if Ang tries to help you," I tell him, handing back his credit card, making sure not to touch his fingers. "That's a nasty burn she got."

"Making cobbler or something for a client," Ryan says. "She's such a klutz."

"Kiss her for me," I say, and he winks at me as he leaves.

Next Tuesday she has a cut above her eye. Not a deep one, but bruised and swollen, the kind of cut someone would get from banging her head against a cupboard door. The kind of cut someone would get if hit by a fist with a heavy ring on one finger. Ryan still wears his high school class ring on his right hand.

She can't remember how she got it, really she can't. She was downstairs in the storage room, hunting for some old things she'd packed away. She must have hit her head on one of the shelves. *Such a klutz, Sal! You wouldn't believe it.*

"You hit your head pretty hard, if you don't remember." I'm trying to joke, but it tastes like an orange left sitting in the fridge too long, and she doesn't laugh this time.

"It's going to snow this weekend. For real this time," she says.

"That's what they said last weekend. I'll help you cover the azaleas, if you like."

Over the second latte she falls into a reverie, staring at one of the pencil drawings on the wall. "Sal. Do you remember those journals we kept when we were kids? The stories we wrote for each other? The kind of men we said we'd marry?"

"Oh, I remember." Those long summers of endless days spent cycling down country roads through farm fields and forests, swimming in the creek, picnicking by the roadside, camping with somebody's parents and making dads bait the fish hook. Hanging around the putt-putt place, the carnival, or the mall when we got old enough to put on make-up and boys. We never ran out of things to talk about. We never imagined the universe would not graciously bend to our fantasies, like a great magician waving his wand over every girlhood dream.

"You were going to marry James Dean," she says, tapping her mug. The smile doesn't quite lift her mouth.

"Still looking."

"And I was going to marry a European prince who had a house

somewhere in the Mediterranean," she says, glancing down at her hands.

"An art collection and a yacht."

Ryan works for a shipping company. He makes sure the trucks get where they're supposed to go and the drivers get paid. He is rarely seen without jeans and a baseball cap. A steady job, a decent man. He never talks about his family. They've lived together almost three years. It might take this time, and I don't know what I'll do then. I've already promised I'll be maid of honor, though I don't have the build for a bridesmaid.

"Has Ryan said anything?"

She pokes at the whipped cream in her coffee. "No."

For years we wrote in notebooks to one another during dull classes at school and nights the parents kept us at home. I scribbled in one spiral-bound volume on long bus rides to and from matches, and between recitals and performances, she wrote in mine. I composed choose-your-own-adventure stories and she wrote me songs and personality quizzes. One summer we co-authored a novel about us in our twenties. I became a svelte artist named Yvonne. She was a prima ballerina named Angelique. We ran an art gallery and dance studio in New York City. The story revolved around my dangerous affair with an art thief and her falling in love with an Egyptologist. We promised one another we would be buried with those journals so no one else would ever be admitted to our private world.

I gave them to her when I left for college, taking only what fit in my car. The whole stack, dog-eared, scribbled through, perfumed and stickered. I wonder if that's what she was looking for in the storage room. I'm afraid to ask. If she hears anything she doesn't like, Angeline pulls herself in like a rabbit crouching in grass, making herself as small as possible. I'll bet Ryan tells her not to spend so much time with me. He has no interest in our shared past, sealed to him, a cavern covered with hieroglyphs he can't read.

It would take him half his lifetime to know Angeline as I do. But I don't think he even asks the questions.

"He's just waiting for the right moment," I say. "To sweep you off your feet. Maybe once he's got the basement finished. He wants to propose to you there."

She takes a spoon and mashes the whipped cream, turning her drink a muddy brown. "He'd better."

Yvonne was like me, only thinner, with beautiful eyes. Angelique the dancer was fearless and bold, proud of her strong and capable body. She stood up to everyone, her bullying stepfather, her mother's hard-eyed critiques of her face and figure and makeup and clothes and friends. I remember wondering why Angeline would imagine herself differently. To me, she was perfect, complete, ideal. What was there she needed to change?

Angeline goes out of town for a conference and Ryan invites me to shoot pool with the guys. We take turns buying pitchers and running the ancient juke box. When he punches my arm or tousles my hair, the touch is like a brother's, or an old friend's.

"Ang really hit her head on something," I say while he's racking balls for the next game.

"I wasn't there," Ryan says, rolling the triangle across the felt. The twitch at the corner of his eye tells me he's lying.

"You ever going to ask that girl to marry you?"

"Don't rush things, Sal."

"I promise I won't tell her."

He lifts the rack and the balls stay in perfect alignment, poised, ready, pointing at me. "You can't keep a secret from her," he says.

Angeline's face lights up my cell phone at 1:00 a.m. "I need a ride to the emergency room," she says. "I fell. I think I broke my wrist."

I'm already rolling out of bed, sliding my feet into flip-flops. "Ice," I say. "For twenty minutes. Can you grip anything?"

"I can't move it." She's not crying, but her voice is hoarse, as from screaming.

"Possible fracture. Have Ryan wrap it. You have a bandage in the house, right?"

"Ryan's gone." A beat of silence. "He took the car."

"Ice, and don't move it," I tell her, pulling on an old flannel, the cast-off of some James Dean wannabe. "Make sure the door is unlocked." Before she moved in with Ryan, I always had her key.

The drive through the empty streets is dark, fast and slippery. The rain plays tricks on the eyes. Sal to the rescue. It feels good. At the apartment all the lights are on and the door open. Angeline slumps at the kitchen table, icepack around her wrist, a towel wrapped around the ice pack. Her profile holds stiff and dry until she sees me, then tears start channeling her face. No sniffing or redness here; Angeline cries beautifully.

"I just fell," she says. "I put out my hand to catch myself and my wrist snapped like a candy cane. Oh, Sal, it hurts." She bites her lip as I lift her fingers. I've had enough sports injuries to know broken when I see it.

"You'll be all right. We'll go straight to the hospital."

I look around for her jacket. The shoes heaped before the door are all Ryan's; Angeline puts hers neatly away in the closet. Things lie scattered all over the living room: old shirts, magazines, somebody's toothbrush. How can he do this to her? Angeline hates a mess. I pull an afghan off the couch and shake debris from it.

"Where did Ryan go?"

"He didn't say."

So still she sits, with her head up, tilted.

"Did he leave before or after you hurt yourself?"

She won't look at me. She cradles her wrist with her good hand and tries to unfold a Kleenex at the same time. I put the afghan around her shoulders and pick up the box of tissues.

"Ang, how did this happen?"

"Please, can we just go?" She lifts her face and I see the red mark across her cheek. I grab her chin to make her eyes meet mine.

"I'm going to break every bone in his body, and I mean that."

"It happened when I fell. Please, let's just go." Underneath the afghan, her shoulders seem so small.

The ride to the hospital takes place in utter silence, no sound but the thoughtful hum of the heater and the windshield wipers slashing at the rain. I am not allowed into the treatment area with her but politely pointed in the direction of the coffee maker in the lobby. The reading material is a stack of women's magazines with headlines like "How to Make Him Wild for You." I've made a few men wild in my day, and to no good consequence. It helps when you don't know what you want.

After the third mindless sitcom ends, a nurse comes to fetch me. She looks borrowed from the pediatric ward; her coat blooms with teddy bears.

"You're with Angeline?" she asks, smiling, and leads me to a curtained-off alcove where Angeline lies on one of the adjust-a-beds. They've put her in a hospital gown. She has a blanket over her waist and the gown pulled up to expose her stomach. Another woman moves a small paddle back and forth across her smooth belly while they both stare at a tiny, colorless screen. *Internal injuries.* I clench with fear. *Bleeding.* Angeline watches the monitor, eyes round as quarters.

"What is it?"

"Look," Angeline breathes.

I see vague cloudy shapes and a white glob in the middle of the screen. Clouds move and change around it. I look at the paddle: not over her stomach. Lower.

"You're probably about six weeks along," the tech says.

Angeline's face is radiant with sweat and wonder. I feel dumb and a little dizzy, like I just took a body check and can't figure out why I'm on the ground.

"You're pregnant? And you didn't tell me?"

"I didn't know." I see the trace of that cut on her shining face.

"We have to ask the date of last menstrual cycle," the nurse says. "It's standard."

"And I couldn't remember, so they had me take a pregnancy test."

"Oh, Ang." I take her good hand and squeeze it tightly. "Oh, baby." I thought I wasn't ready to be a bridesmaid? This is so much worse.

We stare at the screen in fascination. I'm looking for a head, for limbs, for anything resembling an embryo. "What's that white glob?" I finally ask.

"That's *it*, goof," she says.

After the nurse leaves I help her dress. Her pajama shirt won't fit over the bulky cast so I give her the flannel, smelling of me. The nurse supplies gooey ointment to rub on her face to protect the abrasion from infection, and as I touch the bruised spot, she winces. Now I realize what I felt, all those years ago, when she cut her foot on the rosebush and I saw her blood on the snow. I wanted to scoop up that snow and put it in my pocket. I had hurt her and I wanted to repair her, give her wholeness back to her, if I could.

As I fill out her discharge papers, Angeline stares at the wall, holding her immobile wrist with her good hand. For once I can't read the expression in her eyes.

"Ang," I say as we walk out the sliding doors. "Come home with me."

The words echo like coins dropping into a still pool. I want them to reach out and turn her face to me, put hope in her eyes. But Angeline will always put her head down and endure. All those years when I didn't know her, but she knew me.

"He didn't do anything to me, Sal." She looks me in the eye as I belt her into my passenger seat. "I work with this crap every day. You think I'd put up with it in my home? My space?" Her voice says, *You don't know me at all.*

My hands are shaking so much I can't turn the ignition key. I know her. I know her up, down, and sideways. I know the Angeline of the journals, of our daydreams, the princess I rescued over and over again. Ryan was the one who put her on the raft and started pushing her away. I keep throwing ropes, and one after another they keep breaking, slipping free.

"I'm just saying it's going to be tough for you, with that cast." Hail peppers the roof of the parking garage with fine pellets. It's freezing and she only has that stupid afghan. She turns to look at me, her face as smooth and distant as the moon.

"The baby," I say in desperation.

"It's *his* baby," she answers, holding her wrist. She sounds calm and happy. She is a woman who has just learned she carries a life inside her.

I remember all those times sitting with him while he muttered into his beer. How to make Angeline notice him. Want him. His friends begged her to take him back.

"I wish I could see Ryan's face when you tell him."

She leans her head against the headrest of my passenger seat, closing her eyes, and I see that the painkillers haven't kicked in yet. We are growing lines on our faces, she and I.

"He's trying to leave me," she says.

"What?" I say this over the roar of the engine as it suddenly starts.

"The burn. I was standing at the stove, making soup. He said something about taking a break. I—I took the pan and I threw it at him. Tomato soup everywhere."

I can't look at her. I feed the ticket into the automatic meter, then my credit card. My hands are still trembling.

"The cut—I went after him in the garage. I just—saw red. And not the lumber he had piled on the boat." She touches the cut, briefly.

"And tonight?"

"He told me to call you. Come over. Get some space." She looks at her wrist, strokes the temporary cast. She'll get the real one in a couple of days, when the swelling goes down. "We were in the basement. I ran after him with a drill. And tripped on the stairs." She puts her good hand over her face, cupping the palm over her nose. I can hear her breathing the way she does before she cries.

"He can't do this to me, Sal. Not again. I cannot go through that again."

Carefully I put on my blinker, carefully turn onto her road.

"You can stay with me as long as you need to. I've got the space."

"There's a baby. He can't leave me now." She puts her hand in her lap, head on the headrest. The streetlights slide over her face, one after another, a luminous caress. Dawn is a smoky smudge between houses, the last shreds of darkness gathering under the trees.

We left every light on, but at least I remembered to lock the door. The keys are slick in my cold fingers. Angeline sags against the doorframe, pulling the afghan around her hunched shoulders, over her nose. She walks in like a snail carrying her house on her back.

"I'll stay with you. Sleep on the couch."

"No. Ryan will be home soon. It's okay."

I'll never leave her. But she knows that.

I put her in bed and tuck the covers around her. She feels like a bird, hollow-boned. She holds the tiny ultrasound picture in her hand. She could put it up to her stomach and say, *This is inside me, right here*, and I would not believe her. It is neither possible nor real.

Everything I say to her sounds like a greeting card. *Take care of yourself. Call me if you need anything.* She nods and says she will. I turn off all the lights except the one over the kitchen sink, a nightlight, a welcome home.

Outside the sidewalk stretches for acres, and the freezing rain nicks my skin. How she'd wave when she saw me coming down the country lane, would keep waving as our bicycles closed the distance. During swim championships our senior year I could hear her voice above all the others, screaming my name from the bleachers. Once I had all her dreams written down for me. Now she wants something else, and the drift will continue, wider and bigger, as she floats away to a world I can't imagine. The weight of everything I can't say pins me to my car seat, hands clinging to the steering wheel. I watch the streetlights go off one by one, a telegraph line stretching away from me, and realize the raindrops have turned magically, without my even seeing it, into snow.

THE PRESIDENT IN ROME

June 9, 2007

The President of the United States is learning Italian.

"*Ciao* means hello and goodbye," the aide says as they sit snugged into Air Force One, which finally has clearance to fly from the snarled mess that is Poland's national airport to the equally snarled mess that is Italy's. The President's car, The Beast, waits for them in a private hangar, and a police escort will guide their progress into Rome. The first stop is the American embassy, to set right a few nasty rumors about that trial of the CIA agents who kidnapped a known terrorist and extradited him to Egypt. Then the meeting with Napolitano, Italy's president.

The President is glad he brought The Beast with him, though it is something of a joke among his staff that he refuses to travel without it. The car is so plated and fortified it could survive a bombing. Maybe even a nuclear war.

After meeting with the Italian president and the premier, he has a meeting scheduled with the pope.

"But *ciao* is an informal salutation, to be used with children, acquaintances, and those who are in positions of inferior authority," the aide goes on. He reads from a small book that says *Learn Italian in 60 Minutes* on the front. The lesson has just begun.

"Chow," the President says to Laura. She's pulled the black veil of her hat over her face and is pretending to be asleep. He knows she is pretending because when she is really sleeping, her lips and face relax.

The air conditioning is on in Air Force One. Air in the air, the President thinks. His stomach shifts as the plane finds a new altitude. He still hasn't recovered from the G-8 summit and all that starchy German food. He misses their cook at the White House, who once worked at a Longhorn Grill and can make a steak just how the President likes it. The President is not a food snob.

"However, in your case, Mr. President, you'll want to use *buongiorno* in the morning, which means good morning, and *buonasera* in the afternoon, which means—"

The President presses an orange buzzer and a crew member appears.

"Sonia—it's Sonia, right? I'd like you to bring me a Diet Coke."

"Right away, Mr. President." Only after she dematerializes does he realize her glossy name badge reads Jackie.

"To say please you say *per favore*, and excuse me is *scusi*. If you are greeting a superior, you would say—"

"Leonard." The President gives his aide the look he uses with pushy reporters. Leonard's ears move back as his eyes widen. "It is Leonard, right?"

"Yes, Mr. President?"

In his younger days, the President would have called a man like Leonard a drip. His girls use the term wanker. The President went to the Internet to find out what that word means. It is much the same.

"This is a diplomatic mission," the President says. "They are welcoming the leader of the free world. I think everybody can manage to speak American to me."

"Of course, the embassy will provide interpreters, but as a matter of politeness—"

Where was the State Department getting these kids from? Back when he was in the military, they didn't argue with those in authority. They showed the proper respect.

"Leonard," the President says, holding up his Diet Coke. "I am the President of the most powerful country in the world. Nobody is superior to me."

Leonard and the rest of the stooges decide to cancel the visit to some place in Trastestervie—Trastaveery—the President couldn't pronounce it and gave up trying. The AIDS support group would come to the Embassy instead. The President grabs his stomach as The Beast lurches to a halt on its way to Napolitano's house. Damn this Roman traffic. He doesn't say the words aloud because Laura doesn't like it when he uses strong language. The escort hasn't arrived yet; more security snafus. There is a large anti-war protest marching through the city. His motorcade will avoid the protest route.

Nobody can trust these Italians to do anything right, but his security advisors don't have enough leash to go ahead and do their own thing. They should be able to, in the President's opinion. Furthermore, the American government should be able to extradite terrorists wherever they want and torture them as much as necessary. Who was tortured on September 11, huh? Americans were fighting, again, to make the world safe for everybody. Their boys were dying over there. Just yesterday, after another roadside bombing outside of Baghdad, the President made another red dot in his book of crimes that the terrorists were responsible for. Every red dot represented a U.S. casualty in Iraq. Somebody had to pay for all this.

"Can't someone do something about this terrible traffic?" the President says, interrupting another aide—not Leonard this time—who is explaining their approach to the Vatican. Something about a secret passage and a detour to avoid the crowds. "And can someone please turn on the air conditioning?"

"It's already on, dear," Laura says, fanning herself with her purse. The veil is again in place.

"We'll be out of this in a jiffy, sir," another dark-suited, well-groomed aide—not Leonard—says. "We're just waiting for the police escort."

They'd better be out of this whole place in a jiffy, the President thinks. Depart Rome on Sunday, a quick breeze through Albania where he will be honored as a hero, and then finally, thank God, he and Laura could go home. To American food, American electricity, American highways, and American bathrooms with all the hot water and shower pressure you could ask for. The President remembers one thing about his first trip to Italy, a pleasure trip before 9/11 and the world blew up. Those were the honey days, when he was new to the presidential game and Laura still enjoyed traveling and rich food didn't make her too tired and bloated to want sex. He remembers the cleavage and jewelry of Italian women, and the trickle of water they called a hotel shower. Okay, so those are two things, but still.

"Things were better back in Berlusconi's day," the President reminds everyone. "And now this stinking Communist government."

"Sir," one of the aides says, shifting his eyes to the front of the car where a Swiss Guard, a goodwill ambassador from the pope, sits next to the driver. The man is young and desperately handsome, a Fellini-style, pouting, Italian kind of handsome. The President had been something of a blade back in his day. Too bad the boy's job required such a dopey costume.

"They just don't get it," the President says, putting a finger under his very uncomfortable tie. "Accusing the U.S. of secret kidnappings? Putting our agents on trial, when they work hard in the defense of our country? Of course there are secret kidnappings," the President snaps. "This is a war on terror, not a school assembly."

He hears the squeal of an approaching police motorcade. European sirens are the single most grating sound he has ever heard, except when Laura started grinding her teeth in her sleep.

"We understand that, Mr. President," one of the non-Leonards says.

"Do you? Does anybody really understand? We are working," the President says, pulling at his tie, "to make our country safe. Safe from Communists, from terrorists, and all those other crackpots who hate democracy."

"Napolitano is still our ally, sir," one of the aides, the female, speaks up. Oh, was she going to start this again? They had to bring her because she was fluent in at least eight European languages, but she got on the President's nerves. She contradicted everything he said. She wouldn't last long on this job, the President predicted. Everybody these days spoke English; they had to.

Only his Secretary of State really understood what he was doing for the country, for the American people. The President wishes she were here. Condy, who he had to appoint because she was a black woman, had turned out to be his rock. Just yesterday she said in a news interview that history would highly rank this President and his accomplishments. It was what he needed to hear before the presidential candidate debates began and the bullshit really began to fill the air. Communist sympathizers were not what he wanted to hear, not about and not from.

Thank Jesus he has a meeting with the pope. The one man he can count on to see sense about abortion, stem cell research, and gay marriage. Shoot 'em all and let God sort 'em out, as they said back in Texas. Though of course he was speaking metaphorically. John Paul II had been a shithead about the Iraq War, too, but the President trusted that this pope would be more reasonable. He had lived in the wake of Hitler, of Mussolini. He knew what terrorists did to a country.

The President grabs his stomach again as the car jolts into motion. The aides didn't get it; nobody got it. Everybody had a finger to point, but the American people got to sleep well at night because the President was there, making the tough decisions. Nobody worked harder than he did.

There is some problem with the route, and the President's motorcade, on its way to the Vatican City, passes a pocket of protesters. The driver immediately turns onto a side street, but not before the President sees, through the darkened windows, the mass of people in the piazza. A sea of human heads throngs the square, arms and signs waving like antennae. The fountain in the center is indistinguishable under its encrustation of human life, dangling rainbow-colored flags that say "pace."

"That's the gay flag," the President says. "Don't they know that's the gay flag? What is this, gays against war? Gays about to run a marathon?"

Nobody in the car gets the joke. The President is accustomed to having no one understand his sense of humor. Not even Laura, who lost hers sometime after he bought the Texas Rangers and before his second term as governor. Laura loved being the patroness of a Major League baseball team.

"It's pronounced *pah-chay*," Leonard says. "It means peace."

"I had Latin at Andover," the President snaps.

The next square doesn't have any banners: it has posters. "No Bush, no war," they all read in English. Some of the posters, quite unimaginatively in the President's opinion, have photographs of him with devil's horns penciled in. He used to see the same posters in demonstrations at Harvard.

"Hey look, it's me," the President says, pointing again. "They made a doll of me." It's like being at a carnival.

"Romans love a spectacle," the female aide says. She peers out the window as if nervous about the crowd. Why should she be nervous? They have the best security force in the known world protecting them.

"I guess that's why there were all those combats with gladiators and such," the President says, reminding them that he knows more than they do about Rome.

He sees a torch moving through the crowd and cranes his head to watch as the car turns another corner, where policemen at the end of the street frantically wave their arms. Don't Italians know how dangerous it is to have open flame in a crowded area?

The torch comes in contact with the doll of the President, and it catches fire.

"Oh, my God," he hears Laura say on the back of his neck.

One of the non-Leonards throws himself in front of the window, but it is too late. The President sits back in his seat and clutches his stomach.

"Why in God's name," he begins, and then falls silent.

The air-conditioning in The Beast pumps full blast, making the car bitingly cold. He feels nauseated.

"It's something Romans do all the time," the female aide says to Laura. "I wouldn't worry about it."

"Of course we're not worried about it," the President snaps. As soon as they get back to the Oval Office, he is going to speak to someone. This young woman does not know how to do her job. As the girls would say, she is getting up in his grill.

The President is quite sure all the jolting from the cobblestones is going to make him vomit. Goddamn ancient Roman streets. This life is ruining his health. Sometime between his first term as President and the second election, his hair lightened from a dark and rather attractive grey to grey-white. When he looks in the mirror each morning he sees new and deeper lines of frustration. They are the prize for all he accomplished, as Condy says. For being one of the most influential leaders in history. He brought down the Taliban; he executed Saddam Hussein.

"I am not a terrorist," the President says.

They come to the pope's private audience chamber using the secret passage popes have used for centuries. At the end of it stands a gate locked with a heavy chain and a padlock the size of a man's hand.

"This is unacceptable," the head Secret Service agent says. "This is completely and totally unacceptable." He turns to the Swiss Guard who is with them and makes a gesture. The annoying female aide begins speaking in rapid Italian. The Swiss Guard shrugs, a half-smile on his sullen face. Apparently he shares the President's view about uppity women.

"When in Rome," the President says jauntily. Again no one cracks a smile. His girls would appreciate the joke, the President knows.

Leonard turns them around and starts leading them down another passage. "We go this way," he says.

Leonard is dead wrong. He brings them out to the main square of Saint Peter's, into a solid, moving mass of people. They stand in what looks like a military formation. The President steps back quickly.

"No one is supposed to see me!" he reminds his careless staff.

"We just need to duck in this side door," Leonard says. He speaks to a uniformed man who stares at them in surprise and reaches for the radio hooked to his belt loop. Leonard seems to have rather rapidly absorbed the *Learn Italian in 60 Minutes* book.

"This is the biggest mess I have ever seen in my life," the President says.

"We would never be this inefficient in America."

Leonard is finally right; it is only a short distance. They walk under the cool colonnade which smells of mildew and pigeon shit. Next to one of the columns, a small girl sits on the ground in a bright red dress. She plays on a small Fisher Price keyboard, a sequence of notes without a melody. Her smile shows a long gap between her upper teeth.

"*Ciao!*" she calls when she sees them approaching and starts a string of senseless babble. She has soft dark hair cupped behind her ears and the most piquant eyes the President has ever seen. His daughters killed him when they were little and looked up at him with their big dark eyes, but this girl's eyes are bottomless. She must be one of those gypsies he's heard of. They let them run free everywhere here, begging and stealing. She would have a safe warm home and foster parents if she lived in America. To the President she suddenly represents the plight of the whole world, all its desperate and homeless who have nothing to dream about, nothing to hope for. He digs in his pocket for his money. A single American coin might change the course of this girl's entire life.

"Chow," the President says, bending forward to put a quarter in her little tin cup.

The girl looks up at him and her smile freezes. The President sees her whole face change. She isn't a pretty gypsy child; she is a wizened gypsy hag. With one motion she snatches at her cup of coins and leaps to her feet, keyboard tucked under her arm, skirt swirling around her. She skitters sideways like a crab and turns her head to spew a string of useless sounds at them. Then she spits.

The small cluster of spit, gleaming in the Roman afternoon, arcs through the colonnade and lands exactly where she was sitting, right at the President's feet.

The President straightens and puts his quarter back in his pocket.

"I guess you can't help people who don't want to be helped," he says with the jaunty smile he uses for the reporters who are not pushy. The smile of the warm, concerned man that the American public gets to see.

Laura is looking at him. For once she's pushed her veil back from her face.

As they walk down the guarded passage to the pope's private apartments, with Swiss Guards flanking them before and behind, the President remembers something else from an earlier trip to Italy. It must be in the Vatican museum, someplace close to here. It is a painting of St. George slaying the dragon, and as the President recalls, it fills a whole room. Such a glow there was in that room when he first saw that painting, flushed with a light that threw every line into high relief, made every color vibrant and clear. The scene called to him, drawing him in, reminding him to be armed for the battle to come. Every once in a while in the dark of night that painting comes to his mind, the look St. George wears as he faces the enemy. They are men who never surrender, the St. Georges of the world. Medieval knights and Texas cowboys: two men who never back down from a fight.

At the door to the pope's apartments, the President pauses while four of his Secret Service agents and part of the Swiss Guard go in. He waits a moment, accustomed to this protocol. There will be time for the media to enter and snap pictures of all the glad-handing, and then time for him and the pope to have a serious talk. The President hears again the beat of helicopter blades passing overhead, the police monitoring the protesters. He pats his pocket to make sure he has his Rolaids, and he straightens his tie. Then the door opens and the President steps forward to meet a man with a job almost as hard as his own is, a man who like him is one of the pillars who holds up the world.

RIVER BOTTOM

She sat on the deep wooden porch in the chair her grandfather had made, and she rocked. The evening clouds, dark in their underbellies, clumped and hurried toward the line of beech trees lining the creek. The insects hummed and the birds chittered and the frogs croaked nervously, and once in a while the big garrulous *ga-THUMP* of the bullfrog belched through the other noise.

From the bedroom inside the house she heard the same sporadic hacking, the guttural expulsion and then the dry wretched scratching for air. Behind it was the rattle she'd heard before, when the grandfather who'd shaped this chair had lain, years ago, in that very bed, choking up lungs tarred black by a life in the coal mines. When she heard that rattle, she came out on the porch to wait.

No one worked in the coal mines anymore; now they blew up mountains and scraped the top flat as an angel cake, pushed the blasted rubble and the twisted roots of the great oaks and spruces into the valleys, suffocating rivers, towns, a whole way of life. Fast, maybe. But not clean. Death never was.

Some time ago, before the belly of the sun reached the far blue hill, he'd stopped calling her name, ceased the faint, desperate cackle for "Ell—Ell—Ell." Soon it would all cease, all of it. The spitting of his saliva and the stomach lining poisoned by lead, nicotine, the many strange compounds with their haunting names that he had breathed by choice and by lack of choice all his life. The querulous "Nell! Get in here, you good-for-nothin'!" The curses, the hand flat and hard against her ass or the back of her head, or pointed, as it had once or twice, toward the shotgun leaning behind the door. The hands so eager and fumbling in their cold softness on her wedding night, when she was bought and unwrapped like a slab of meat. All the times that heavy imprint had come with a "Dammit, woman!" or "Why you make me do these things?" or "Wipe that look off your face, or you'll get it agin." You could hardly blame a man for doing what he'd seen other men do all his life, for doing what he was driven to do. But you could hardly blame a woman, could you, if the bruises went deep and lodged there, waiting.

She wasn't unchristian; she'd left a glass of water by the bed. He couldn't reach it. It wouldn't help. Tomorrow she would look on a new sunrise, a new land, the land that had belonged to her family for a hundred years and would now belong only to her, the fields, the creek bottom, the ancient trees not yet gutted by disease or rot or bulldozers dowsing for coal. She listened to the dry scratching voice and the way it blended with the frogs, a chorus of nature, no sentient thought behind it but the desperate wish to survive. She listened the bullfrog bellow and stop. She rocked. In a little while the faint, damp, muddy river smell would come drifting up on the fog.

HAPPINESS

At twilight, two heavenly messengers appeared on my doorstep.

"We've come to bring you happiness," they said.

I thought about it. "I'm already happy."

Many years ago, I lived in a hot land, and I lived alone. Every few weeks I cleared the ivy from my yard and planted sunflower seeds. Each time, something ate them: a bird, a squirrel, a dog. But I looked around me at the live oaks trailing their veils of lichen, and I thought, *life is possible*. So I kept planting seeds, and look you, it grew into this: my crumbling doorstep upon which you stand, this my green patch of yard, this my red maple bleeding sap. My house with the green shutters, my car in the driveway. I have every creature comfort, yet still I sleep under a lofty tree, with the baby bears safe in their bed. How could I not be happy?

"We would like to offer you conversation," they said. "We bring you a fairy tale. We can show you the path into the Enchanted Forest."

Oh, you darlings, I wanted to say. *Oh, you dears*. Once, I lived in a fairy tale. Every day I climbed the beanstalk, and every day I turned into a giant, shouting and stomping and threatening to eat my children. So I hopped off the beanstalk and walked to the town and took up a trade. I take the papers and read the words and tell people what they say, and they give me small scraps of paper in return for my knowledge, and I use them to buy bracelets and coffee and shoes. And every day I am glad to have the scraps of paper instead of the fairy gold.

The angels wore shoes, wingtips, and they wore light men's jackets like my father as a young man in the picture of him with his first Mustang. They wore ties and their white shirts covered the nubs of their wings. They spoke of the blinding white gown and a rain of riches, the yellow brick road to the Emerald City, where the chosen dine off gold plates and bathe in holy water and wrap themselves in silks and luxuries that slide pure from the palm of God.

"Oh," I said, and opened my hands. What I wanted to say was, *It is not for you to save me, you sweet-faced children.* Under my sweaty shirt I bear the stripes of penance and humiliation, and on my door is the blood of the sacrifice. My God sends locusts and asps to test his chosen. My God sends an angel with a flaming sword. My God would have me bow on scabbed knees beside the other wretches, would have me know that He holds his hand over the heads of my beloveds and what He giveth, He may take away. I have not been given the wide smooth road to riches. I have been brought into the wilderness to feast on herbs and nettles, and every rock in my path shines with holiness.

"We wanted to remind you of the season," they said kindly. The season of birth, and birth again.

"I know something about birth," I told them. Five years ago in the time of spring I felt a twinge in my belly and I found a thread. I pulled on the thread, and at the end I had to pull very hard, and out popped a baby girl with a flower blossom face and petal hands. Three years ago, on Easter, I lay down on a table and a magician waved his hands over my navel and out came a fat baby boy, black-haired and shrieking. Never again, when you have seen such wonders, is happiness like a balloon, untethered. Happiness is a stake to the heart, and in comes in bolts that leave you pierced, the air blowing through.

They looked at one another, and then at me. I could see they had not expected this: to come to the cottage with a message of hope and find the crone who is becoming the wise woman, the witch who would entertain angels. They looked behind them for the trail of crumbs. I wanted to take their hands, these walkers on the paths of truth. I wanted to stretch my hands over their heads in a blessing, but would they take it from me, a sweaty woman in workout clothes, damp from the children's bath? We stood there beaming at one another as I saw then their gift: to bring me to stand for the first time that day on my porch and smell the spring air at dusk. To see the red buds on the maple. To remember that the sky I see over my head reaches into the infinite, and it shelters many many many other heads besides mine.

"Thank you," I said as they unfurled their wings. "I'm happy."

They floated away into the evening, smiling, and this time, I think they believed me.

THIS IS HOW TO HOLD

This is how to hold a baseball: light and easy, knuckles curving around the sphere, balancing it on your fingertips. Think about your wrist dropping back and snapping forward, your arm a grand arc, the ball hurtling like a small planet straight at the catcher's face. Don't think about Billy Johnson, that jerk, scowling from the dugout, got a girl on his team. Breathe from your stomach. Think of playing catch in the summers with your brother, Dad in the middle, hayfield stubbled around your ankles, the smell of clover in a wet dusk. Think of the thump and the chain of tingles when the ball slams into your glove. Look at the strike zone and let go lightly. The laces stay printed on your fingertips.

This is how to hold your new kitten: one hand under the soft rubber-band belly, the other stroking its fur backwards, making the hair stand up in frantic tufts. Watch it turn its head and hiss at you, milk teeth bared like miniature fangs. This brings out something feral in you, your own cat nature. The small teeth dig pin-like into the soft flesh of your hand, leaving a ring of watermelon seeds, so tiny and desperate.

This is how to hold the arabesque allongée position, while Madame bellows at you to tighten, hold still: extend, back arched, leaning forward, the leg behind you reaching back and up, something not altogether attached to you. Wobble slightly on the tips of your toes. Imagine yourself a willow reed, hopeful with grace, bending in the wind. You are one of Degas's ballerinas, blurred, pink and wistful, a thing of beauty. This is the way you were meant to move, you whisper to yourself, while Madame keeps correcting, her hands like iron clamps on your ankle, hold *still*.

This is how you hold the steering wheel: hands at two o'clock and ten o'clock, gripping the plastic, white-knuckled, sweaty, your fear scented with the chili-pepper breath of the driving instructor barking from the passenger seat: turn left, parallel park, and isn't it a shame such a nice car doesn't come with a turn signal? Do not cry. Do not lift your hands to wipe sweaty palms on your jeans. If you can do ballet you can get your driver's license, why should one be any harder than the other? Pretend you are dancing with the car, a precise choreograph of turns and glides and *there* you remembered to use your blinker. Do not think that you are driving a tin can, wielding the wheel like a weapon, one ton of possible vehicular manslaughter under your hands. Press gently on the accelerator, gently on the brake. You are careful, see? You are careful. When you climb out of the car your legs wobble the way they do after a recital. Your fingers cramped in the shape of claws.

This is how to hold your college diploma: lightly and with pride, flushed and a little nervous, so intent on not tripping that you don't actually hear if the dean remembers to say *cum laude*, rewarding all those dim hours in the library. Turn and smile your blinking eyes at the camera as the chancellor takes your hand, turn and smile at your parents as you proceed down the steps. Wave this small piece of paper like a banner, a victory, a triumph of things endured. Years later you will find it on a shelf at your parent's house, serene and accomplished in its faux leather case, powdered with tiny grey dust.

This is how to hold your lover: one moment mad with passion, the next dropping like a star into your own private universe, distant and remote, as though your body has not absorbed his entirely, as though the texture of his skin does not linger on your hands. This is the feel of regret, a stone in your stomach, when you think that of all you have wished for in your life this is the thing you want most—his eyes on you with a look of love—but you are only the janitor, brushing around the edges of him, polishing a marble statue. You are not the sculptor, the one who can animate his heart. Hold his hand lightly, fingers tangled like your hair when you lean your head against his shoulder. Let him see your desire. This will make him feel strong. Do not let him see your need. Keep this hidden in the butter box, behind the broom in the utility closet. Let go lightly, without tears, without sending the accusatory letters that you compose for weeks afterward, full of one-sided arguments and justifications. Sometimes it does not matter how hard you hold.

This is how to hold your new nephew: with both hands, pretending he is made of glass. His head bobs like a flower on a stem. Watch his eyes as they watch you, a foggy, unfocused blue. Think how he looks like a toad, his small face puffy at the cheeks and chin. When your brother asks you say he is beautiful, do not say he looks amphibian. Feel the delicate curve of ribs beneath the fuzzy blue sleeper pajamas with the plastic on the feet. Feel the rapid rise of his chest as you hold him against you. All the mysteries of creation have gone into those tiny fingers, the impossibly small fingernails. Pretend when you give him back to his mother that he is still reaching for you.

This is how you hold yourself in what your mother calls your dear-God-seventeen-hundred-dollars wedding dress: graceful as a swan, neck high and shoulders back, your satin sequined train sweeping behind you. You are the lost princess Anastasia, you are Scarlett O'Hara, in this moment you are every beautiful woman in the world. Remember to breathe. Clutch your flowers during the ceremony and try not to think that you are binding yourself to him forever, forever is such a long time; till death parts you is much more acceptable, you can handle death. When you come to him that night like Aphrodite rising from the water he will laugh the same way he did when you first said yes: at once nervous, grateful, and relieved; perhaps he was not sure you would really choose him, after all. The word husband feels like the words 'steamer trunk,' something quaint and devoted and old-fashioned which you never imagined you would possess. Wish sometimes he were a little less adoring and a little more sarcastic. Wish sometimes he would take himself out with the trash. Hold your husband's hand like a familiar treasure, your curves and impressions fitting with his, fingers intertwined like the point and counterpoint of a harmony, a song. It is your favorite song.

This is how to hold your mother's hand as she lies dying: delicately, afraid to damage the tissue-thin skin, the bones standing out among the tremulous veins. Think how these hands have shaped you: the first hands to hold you with love, the hands that bathed you, the hands that slapped you when you repeated the bad words you heard on TV. The hands that stroked your hair when you cried in her lap after that jerk Billy Johnson stood you up for the homecoming dance. The lines on her fingertips bear the combined imprint of two lives wrapped tightly around one another. This is the thing that holds you, a love that suffocates as it supports, never quite finding that balance between freedom and friendship, never fully comprehended until this moment when you stand together in a universe on the brink of extinction. Again these mysteries of life and death escape you, like something remembered from a fever of dreams, leaving you vague and a little restless. This is the shape of your heart: your mother's hands, lying pressed between your own.

This is how to hold your own child: as close to your heart as is possible, so close that you can feel her breath against your skin. Here is your heart taking shape anew, the tiny perfection of each hair on her head, the curve of her lips, her ears, the weblike darkness of her eyelashes against her strawberry cheek. Watch her moving on her own, a tiny and complete personality, a miniature and nascent soul; here, to your astonishment, is a piece of you that has somehow become separate from your own body, self-contained, something you cannot command and yet can claim utterly as yours. She will have your brown hair and her father's blue eyes and you can see her whole life spread before you, a scrapbook of grade school spelling bees, birthday parties and ballet recitals, graduations, her wedding, the day you hold a grandchild against you like this, the tiny heart beating against your chest, not an echo of yours but a whole thing distinct and entirely perfect. Hold her gently, one hand across her back, one hand cupping her head, curved as lightly beneath your fingers as a baseball. This is the reason. This is all that matters: the holding.

BEDTIME FAIRY TALE

—So in the kingdom in the mountains there was this princess—

—No, that's not how it begins.

—You want me to tell you a story, you *demand* that I tell you one, and now you say that's not how it begins?

—It starts, *once upon a time*.

—That's boring. All stories start like that.

—So start it. Once upon a time—

—Don't you want to shake things up a little bit? Don't you want a new story?

—That's how it goes, I'm telling you. Say it right. Once upon a time . . .

—Okay, okay, keep your pants on. Once upon a time—

—There was a dragon.

—Didn't you hear me earlier? The bit about the princess?

—There's always a princess. I want a dragon.

—All right, your highness, what color do you want this dragon to be?

—A green and blue dragon.

—With silvery wings—

—Yes! Now you've got it.

—With silvery wings like a dragonfly—no, don't pout, I'm not making fun of you. It's a green dragon with a blue belly and silver wings, and his name is . . . is . . . aren't you going to tell me what his name is?

—It's your story. You're telling it.

—Okay, the etc. etc. dragon and his name is Pete—

—She.

—Huh?

—Her name. It's a she dragon.

—The dragon is a girl?

—Yuh-huh.

—How come you didn't tell me that earlier?

—I thought you knew.

—Hmmm. Okay. Well, once upon a time there was a she-dragon with a green back and a blue belly and silver wings, and her name was . . . Gertrude.

—Keep going.

—Well, Gertrude is flying around the kingdom one day, and she sees this princess in a tower, and . . .

—And then what?

—This is really hard, you know. Stories. I'm not very good at them.

—You're good. You've got a dragon. That's a start.

—Yeah, sure, beginnings are easy. But the middle and stuff that comes after—that's hard.

—Well, something has to *happen.*

—So what happens in our story? With Gertrude the dragon?

—And the prince.

—Oh, right, there was a prince in there and—wait, didn't I say princess?

—Nuh-uh.

—I thought I said Gertrude was flying around the kingdom and spotted a princess in a tower.

—No, it was a prince.

—What was the prince doing in the tower?

—You tell me. It's your story.

—It's *our* story. You came up with the dragon. Oh, okay. There's a prince in the tower . . .

—Baking cookies.

—Okay, yes, the prince is in the tower baking cookies, and he's stepped out on the terrace because he's getting away from the heat, it's really hot in the kitchen, and besides he's sad because . . . um, because . . .

—Because why?

—Because the cookies are burning?

—No, something worse than that.

—You think of something, then.

—The prince is sad because he fought with his mother.

—Right, the prince fought with his mother because she wants him to take a position on her council and the prince wants to go off to college—or maybe he just wants to go to the waterpark in the next kingdom over.

—No, college is good.

—But how come his mom doesn't want him to go away to college?

—She'll be sad if he's far away.

—Oh, so she wants him close by, which is why she came up with the council idea . . . wait wait wait a minute, what's the matter? Why are you crying?

—It's all his fault!

—What's his fault?

—He made her so angry . . . but he just wanted . . .

—Just to get out for a little bit, try something new.

—Yes.

—And she loves him so much that she's afraid to let him go, that's why she doesn't let him do things sometimes—

—She's trying to keep him safe—

—Yes, she's trying to keep him safe, and she realizes he wants to do things, have new experiences, ride his bike up and down the street sometimes—it's the same for little girls, too. Need to stretch.

—What about Gertrude?

—That's right, almost forgot about her. So Gertrude sees the prince, and he's a little upset, and she says, "What's wrong, prince?" and he says, "It'd be nice to get out every once in a while, you know, go to college—"

—Ride my bike down the street to the park. Alone.

— "Ride my bike, you know, but my mom, the queen, she's not too happy with the idea." So Gertrude says, "What if we got out for a little while, just a little?" and the prince says "What do you mean, Gerty?" and she says, "I'm a dragon, you know. I fly. We can go visit places, like right now," and the prince says, "But Gerty, I've got cookies in the oven"—yeah, you're laughing, you forgot about the cookies.

—I did forget about the cookies.

—You would have left them to burn all to a crisp. Start a fire or something.

—Yuck.

—So here's what happened: Gerty waited until the cookies were done, and the prince packed a couple of cookies in a Ziploc baggie, and then they went flying all over the village, all over the fields and the forests and the baseball diamond—

—And the school—

—Yep, and they flew over the school too, but it was all dark because it was summer recess so no one was at the school, and then after a while Gerty brought the prince home, and he felt a lot better about everything.

—And?

—And they lived happily ever after. The end.

—No no no—you don't get it yet, do you? That's the beginning. The most important part. This is where the story begins.

FLIGHT

I admit it's been a long-awful day for the both of us. What did it I guess was the crayons, though the dinosaurs were close to breaking me. What do you do with Play-doh dinosaurs everywhere, in the pantry, in the fridge, lumps of clay mottled with food coloring—the food coloring for cake, for Easter eggs, now did I say he could use that?—and maybe I spoke sharp but if you had to deal with them, these miniature monsters taking over your house, your son playing with the extinction of humanity, what would you call it? Exercise of imagination? So, I say to him, scratching Play-doh clumps off the counter, creative spirit, right, you going to be an artist, design buildings huh? Go on, be a sculptor, broke and angry all your life. Leave your mark. Better than being a drug addict, I suppose. (Three o'clock: half hour till the roast goes in.)

He waits behind the door to hear me yelp when I pull back my cotton comforter, see the tyrannosaurus rearing up with bared pink teeth, oh I shriek then *you get in here mister* and he cackles and runs off, matchstick legs pumping, shaking the hair out of his face. Can't throttle a kid for being artistic, but devious now, I don't want devious, and how are you supposed to know when it changes? You hatch something in the world and then you live every day with this fear of breaking it, souring it, watching it curdle like old milk, go rotten like eggs. Find me a parenting magazine that runs columns on this.

As I said it was the crayons that did it, opening the oven and finding colored wax melted all over the grill, *Jim dandy!* I told you those crayons were for school, don't go melting them down to make wax birds, sloths, animals for the dinosaurs to eat, when I gave birth to you now there were two ears in your head so why don't you ever listen to me? Little face screws up, he pouts, pulls at his lip, wants to argue and knows he'll lose, disappears into his room. Thinking he hates his mother. How bad his mother is. And me making his dinner, mashing potatoes, mixing biscuits, taking his race cars out of the cutlery drawer and scrubbing out the oven before putting in the dratted roast and if I told him once I told him a thousand times not to play with the oven, do I need to tape a sign on it?

Talking to an empty room. Where is that kid? So it is, so it is: I got all the good ideas, but nobody listening. Turn on the talk show, just for half an hour till his daddy comes home. Teenage daughter yelling at her mother. Everybody knows better than the mother.

Go out to fetch in the dogs and a voice comes from above me. Mom, look at me, I'm a bird. I'm a bird, look at me, Mom. I look. Heart stops. Child on the roof, skinny arms outstretched, every freckle on his face clear as a pebble at the bottom of a pool. Sky behind him summer-bright, as blue as blue ever was. Two-story roof and a twenty-foot fall if he slips, broken bones broken neck a quick snap and everything goes crooked, and I'm not moving but I can't breathe.

Insects buzz in the low grass. Down the street a lawn mower growls across a lawn. Crows call to each other from the tops of the pines. For the love of Mike get down from there, how'd you get tall enough to climb up from the porch, you fall from there you break your neck and I ain't got time to be at the hospital and he's heard this so many times, the scolding, it's all crows to him, he just stands there grinning with his tiny gapped teeth and says I'm a bird, Ma, grinning, a bird. Sweet Jesus. Eighteen hours in labor with that child and he's going to kill himself right here.

That plaid shirt flaps over his bony elbows, arms outstretched, and when did he start wearing his daddy's clothes? Next he'll be wanting to shave. Eight years old and who remembers now how that feels, bones busting out of their body, wanting to move land masses. I can't think what would happen to my heart if I never saw that grin again. At three he was a fat lump who wouldn't leave my arms and one day not too long from now he'll walk away from me on his own legs, all grown into that flannel shirt and making his own potatoes, though he won't mash them the way I do. Stupid permission slip, its pretensions. You tell me how to keep him out of drugs, keep him from suicide, keep him sane and safe and normal and whole. Nobody tells you how to do this, how to stay soft and keep stretching out and out and out, like a giant piece of silly putty, reaching out over all the canyons, the pitfalls, the debris, the little deaths.

The blue sky. The potatoes burning, the oven starting to smell. His daddy home any minute. Crow calls and another answers. We eyeball each other in the silence, he building-tall and me ant-tiny, to blow away in the suddenest breeze.

So I swallow back the heart again, like you do every day. And I smile like we're strolling on a sidewalk and I say to him, how's the view up there, mister, how you feeling? And he says oh, I feel fine, Ma, I got wings. *Yes you do, baby. You do.* And I think if he jumped now I'd catch him and he'd come into my arms like a gift all over again, bones as hollow as a reptile or a bird's, something too, too fragile to hold.

WELCOME TO LULUTHELESBIAN.COM!

Lulu the Lesbian's Advice & Chat:
Your Peek Behind the Lavender Curtain

April 24

So, girls.

Have you noticed all the new fashions this spring are in pink? What is this, the 1950s? It frightens me, ladies, it truly does, to see what the hetero world is doing to its women. This is third wave feminism, my friends and followers: we are now free to express our inner pinkdom? We can be frilly, frou-frou, giggle and speak in high voices, yet still expect to be taken seriously by the adult population? Wear skirts that show everything from Florida to Canada and still expect that the people with whom we conduct business will judge and value us on the basis of our creative abilities and intellectual worth? Maybe I'm just an old-fashioned second wave lesbian, but I think there is a danger in flirting with these stereotypes. It's violence against women, to turn us all into bubble-headed bubble-gum girls. The fashion industry wants to keep us all Lolitas because the adolescent market is one of the few segments of the market that reliably continues to grow. Plus, if we grow up to be solely and obsessively concerned with our grooming and appearance, we have no time for politics, activism, education, executive offices, and the fine arts, thus leaving the important things in the hands of the capable gents. Does this not have a vaguely putrid odor to you, my chickadees?

So here is Lulu's question for the day: what shall we do, ladies and low-lying lurking males (and I know you're out there using female handles as your log-in names—your vote doesn't count since naturally you want to *see* Florida and Canada, due to that uncontrollable Y chromosome I keep hearing about). Are we to relax and let the invisible hand of consumer-guided capitalism control the market, however that is supposed to work? Are we to freely purchase and jauntily wear the ridiculously-sized synthetic materials produced in southeast Asian sweatshops for us, are we to blithely and without guilt continue to purchase the beauty products we know to be made of non-renewable resources and tested on animals? Should we wildly and unconditionally celebrate our beauty and youth while we have them and while they *are* still so rated so highly by our hip, shallow, ever-more-youthful ultra-modern society? Shall we fulfill the promise of our promiscuous suppliers, advertisers, and other media personnel and engage in (safe) sex at every opportunity as a healthy distraction from the other things going on in the world, say, poverty, hunger, genocide, and disease?

Or, ladies, do we resist, with every fiber of our beings, this new form of oppression? Are we or are we not—as lesbian, bi, trans, flex, abstinent, ascetic, questioning, or eternally uncategorized—eternally excluded by and therefore the declared enemies of the American cult of Woman? Should your own Lulu, hard as it may be, determinedly march right past all the lacy and feathery and winky-blinky things in the window of Pookie's Pockets and make her way to her the reliable, earth-friendly, multi-million-dollar corporations of REI and EMS?

Write your thoughts below; you know I read all posts, unless, of course, they are stupid.

Awash in, drowning, going under for the third time in pink,

Lulu

April 26

All right, then.

I guess I know who reads *this* column. I should get a domain called bubblehead.com and host my column there. Are you *serious*, Angel from Albuquerque, when you tell me that your super-short ultra-pink rubber mini skirt makes you *feel like a woman*? Well, what do you feel like any other part of the day, when you're in your fuzzy pajamas or naked in the shower? What are you then—an ambulatory, sensory-driven piece of meat?

Don't you really mean to tell me that said mini-skirt makes you feel exposed and caricatured, conforming to the preposterous and biologically impossible measurements that a completely hostile cultural mindset tells you is what a *real* woman looks and feels like? Are you honestly going to let the cable networks and Hollywood and the evil advertisers force you into a life of perpetual insecurity, unhappiness, and psychic pain that can only be briefly remedied by the products they want you to buy? I will say to you, all you little Lolitas—because I am writing to you now; you will be the stewardesses of fourth-wave feminism, you will have to introduce a new way for women-loving women to live and love and thrive in the world—I will say to you as Madonna says in that fabulously uplifting song from *Ray of*

Light, travel down your own road.

And if you don't know yet who you are, or what your path is, or what or who you love—if you are still finding this out, as the project of adolescence, as the project of your college years, as the on-going project of your post-college years as your darling Lulu is starting to realize (will all of the twenties be consumed with this task? Possibly)—if, as I say, you are still learning your boundaries and claiming your passions and discovering what truly moves you and what you may leave behind (did I come up with this poetic sentiment on my own, or did I get this from Madonna, too?): do not, I beg of you bubbleheads all, do *not* let Revlon, *Cosmopolitan,* or Hollywood make these decisions for you. And if you eventually find that you must keep your subscription to *Cosmo,* just to fully witness the madness in the world, please flee the latest tasteless teen flicks and gravitate toward actresses of more substantial worth, like Drew Barrymore or Sandra Bullock, who at least have senses of humor (and are, my God, so downright sexy it makes a girl's stomach hurt to watch them).

Though it occurs to me, upon consideration, that I really can't make a fair and impartial decision without experimenting in both arenas. So, dear reader, if it makes you happy, I will fairly and judiciously dabble with this frivolous consumer culture. I will buy myself some of the pink underwear on display at Victoria's Secret and see if it makes me feel like a *woman,* or anything perhaps resembling a woman. It's been pretty quiet in Lulu's bedroom since Elena and I broke up (and if you're new to the column, you *must* read the story of how Elena CHEATED on me with the 6'4" WNBA guard she met at the game I TOOK HER TO—see the beginning of the break-up story in "When the Beast is in Your Bedroom," November 11 of last year). Maybe I need new lingerie to attract some sex into my life.

Cheerfully on her way to the mall,
Lulu

April 28

Bonjour, mes petites:

So Harvey, whom we all know and dutifully love as the editor of the hip and snappy entertainment e-zine *Got That!,* Harvey who hosts this column and keeps Lulu in snickerdoodles as well as her over-priced one-bedroom apartment downtown, tells me I have to tone it down a little. He thinks I'm alienating readers with my acidic tone. (*Am* I alienating you, dear readers?

Such was never my intent.) He reminds me that this is an advice and chat column for those of the alternative lifestyle demographic. I have pointed out to Harvey what is obvious for the rest of us, that fashionable young lesbians, or shy closeted lesbians, or questioning lesbians, or any sort of lesbians at all are still vulnerable to the rapid fire of the mainstream media, and I feel it is my duty, as the old and wise, as the been-there-done-it-twice survivor, to share my wisdom to those first setting their steps upon this walk of life.

But, as my readers remind me, women (and I'm not forgetting you lurking Y chromosomes out there—I'm onto you, whoever and wherever you are) of all ages and persuasions read this column. Lulu's Peek Behind the Lavender Curtain was never, *ever* meant to be exclusionary, folks. In the eight years that I've had this blog (though it's true your Lulu has only in recent years found a home with *Got That!*, who obligingly pays for our little domain and all our webmastering services), we have always been generously, vigorously open to viewpoints of all colors of the rainbow. Lulu's not leaving anybody out of the love. It's cold and dark enough out there in the mainstream world, where all that glitters turns out to be that Victoria's Secret body glitter that brushes right off your skin anyway.

Still a little acidic, but as always right,

Lu-the-Lu

May 1

Aloha!

It's a brand-new month, girlfriends, and as you shake off the winter flab and the cold-weather doldrums, it's time to get some things clear. This is addressed particularly to you, Lacey of Lodi, and the dim-witted harassers who keep calling you a LUG. (Lesbian until graduation, for those of you blessedly unaware of this snide and denigrating term.) First of all, you don't *want* to be in that sorority, girl. Why would you want to surround herself with a hundred little sucking-piranha mouths, biting away at you and telling you who you are is not good enough? All sororities are good for these days, I hear, is for binge drinking, blacking out, and waking up in a scatter of used condoms not even knowing who or how many had their way with you the night before.

Please don't do this to yourself. You are far, far too precious; you must protect the jewel that is you. Go to the next meeting of your campus

LGBTSA, find a mentor, and learn how to thumb your nose at all the people telling you you've been seduced by some packaged and romantic idea of female sex that you'll soon de-mystify and outgrow and then abandon for a triumphant (for them) return to the narrow and stifling hetero fold. Don't let them treat you as though your identity is a trend, a fad, an experiment, or a phase you will outgrow. Coming out is hard, I know it; I was with Debbie for nine months before I could identify as a lesbian. (That was the very beginning of the blog, as my most loyal readers will recall; go far, far back to Lulu's beginnings and there Debbie will be.)

By the way, if you *are* a LUG, a word of caution. Nothing, and I mean nothing, is more dangerous and degrading to the political and social interests of us tried-and-true lesbians than to be an exotic fantasy for the hetero mainstream. It's just one more way to tell us we're unnatural, we don't count. Don't add your voice to that majority, Lacey my love. Follow your bliss, and make sure it *is* your bliss, but don't romp through the Lavender World like it's an amusement park. Have a little respect for those of us who live here.

Time to go binge on "The L-word"—

Lu

May 4

Okay, *whoa.*

Apparently Lulu needs to reconsider what she said about sororities. Apparently there are enough of you allies out there who do not fit the binge drinking, blacking out, and waking up in a scatter of used condoms paradigm and resent the implication that you do. Allow me to tender my sincerest and most humble apologies.

Of course a sorority is a sister-love-fest. Of course I heartily and enthusiastically support any organization that allows girls to establish whole and worthy and deeply emotionally intimate relationships with other girls. I admit I've been brainwashed by images of sororities as squadrons of silicone-implanted chicklets insanely giggling and wearing identical outfits that make it impossible for any of them to evolve an individual personality, much less raise their IQ (*House Bunny* being, of course, the exception—and if you haven't seen Anna Faris on rollerskates yet, you must).

Of course the backstabbing and competitiveness are just stories made up by the jealous; of course sororities help combat and do not promote the self-esteem issues that lead to eating disorders, self-mutilation, or suicide. Clearly I speak out of ignorance, having never had such a fantastic opportunity when I was in college, and I suppose my contempt really is a thin disguise for the envy I felt for the bleached-blonde clique of girls who filled the back row of my history classes and spent the entire lecture period painting their nails and passing notes written on scented pink paper.

I am an ogre, an insensitive beast. Perhaps I only turned to lesbianism because I am a secret sorority failure. I suppose it was a longing for sisterhood that led me into Debbie's arms and not any brilliancy and beauty and complete sexiness of the girl herself.

Tell the Olympic hosts that snipe-hunting is back in the list of events this year,

Lu-hoo-Lu

May 11

Hello my loves,

I'll say this for the Mary-Kate-and-Ashley industrial complex: for as much horror I feel over being forced to publicly witness the very painful walking emptiness of these two media-created girly-girls, whoever is choosing the colors for their nail polish line really knows her stuff. I'm crazy about these colors. In fact, it gave me the idea of what to get Rox and Stacey for their anniversary: I put together a wifesaver pedicure kit, complete with a selection of polishes which, if they don't like, they can give back to me.

Ah, Rox and Stacey—now there's a true love story for you! How unfair that my beautiful cousin Stacey, who should get the looks in the family, the rich still-married parents, and the graduate fellowship to the University of Minnesota to study psychology should also have an adoring and totally committed partner in the form of Rox, who is a bombshell in every sense of the word: gorgeous, smart, funny, and so down-to-earth that she creates her own gravitational field. You can't help but feel your heart hurt a little when you sit in their cozy living room, amid a jungle of flowers and tasteful Art Nouveau reproductions, listening to them tell stories about picking out the new furniture set and watching them kiss each other after opening each new gift to celebrate their first full year of living together. Everybody should get to be that happy, you start to think, and then you come home to your apartment which all of a sudden seems so empty despite the terrible mess. Makes you wonder if maybe you should get a plant.

Though the day was not, unfortunately, perfect, since I continue to receive mail for this William Harkin character, known elsewhere in this column as Willy the Wildebeest. The name should be self-explanatory. Willy, as you are no doubt aware, has been the bane of my existence since he moved in four weeks ago. First there was the parking misunderstanding, then the packing boxes he left in the hall for two days in a row, and now the ongoing mail issue, not to mention several elevator rides where the conversation has been painfully banal. Of course being a girl-lover doesn't mean being a man-hater, but really, some men are idiots.

Here's to Rox, Stacey, and a solitary evening with a self-mixed mango martini,

Miss Lonelyhearts-Lu

May 15

Guess what, girls:

Lulu had a moment this morning with Peggy. You all know Peggy, the Pilates instructor at my all-women gym—yes, that gym, the one you go to when you don't want to be hit on by men.

Now, straight girls, don't get all weirded out that the lesbians are ogling you; we're much more discreet than that. I have *never* leered at a woman at the gym. Except, of course, Peggy. But Peggy is a different story. I beg the pardon of readers who have pointed out that I speak of Peggy as though she is nothing more than a set of breasts. If, as Tommy from Tuscaloosa has pointed out, in describing her beautiful, perfectly-symmetrical set of size-B mammary glands as "bouncing under her racer-back with eloquent grace," or describing the cleavage that forms when she's working on her obliques as "entrancing," or saying of that day of my first introduction to spinning, thanks to a strategically placed question that allowed me five valuable minutes alone with her, that her "pert nipples smirk up at the sky" I am indeed, as Tommy says, being crass and reductive, speaking of her as a set of body parts, exactly what women have always complained about men for doing, I offer, of course, the most abject apologies.

But really, dear reader—if you could see these body parts! Peggy has the most lovely ankles, the most interesting knees. Her flexing shoulders could make anyone drool, and your Lulu is particularly susceptible to shoulders. She's short, which is not my usual type, but so wide-set, so deeply brown are her eyes, so intent and direct is her gaze when she is talking to you about your form that you there and then vow your form will be forever imperfect, just so you can draw her to your side to correct you.

So, as you can see, I adore Peggy on the basis of more than her body. I am not a predatory lesbian, as you know; Lulu is not just out for anything she can get. Lulu is about forming deep relationships and lasting friendships (the break-up with Elena notwithstanding, since we're currently not speaking to each other due to some touchy disagreements in trying to sort out what belongs to whom in our respective DVD collections). But the best romances, naturally, are friendships that also include frequent, vigorous, and as-noisy-as-possible sex.

And, if you've been reading this column (as you should! every day!), you know I have yearned for Peggy since autumn, in a distant, soulful, non-leering sort of way, since I was dating Elena, and Peggy was in a committed monogamous relationship with the girl who'd been her best friend since third grade and who had moved away and married a man who graduated with Peggy's class but when they met again at Peggy's high school reunion it was love at first sight (see "All the Good Ones are Taken," last October.)

But then, you'll remember, they broke up. Not in that sort of bouncing-back-and-forth kind of way, where it takes you as long to break up as you actually were in the relationship, but a fairly clean rift—the partner, I heard, reconciled with her husband. Ouch.

Well, girls, you can imagine the thoughts that came to me when I returned to the gym to work off the break-up blues and hopefully work off that little bit of softness that forms around tummy and hips when you're in a happy committed relationship with someone and you don't have to stay quite so lean and tight and hungry since know where your sex is coming from. And then, the magic: I realized that Peggy was teaching a new five-days-a-week Pilates class and I thought, here's my chance!

So there I was, lagging behind the rest of the class, being the last, again, to pack up my mat. I combed my brains for something I could say that would not be lame—like asking her, for instance, where I could buy one of those balls for home workout. But I didn't want to suggest that I would start working out at home and thereby imply that she wasn't a good teacher, since I want her to know I'm thoroughly besotted with her and adore being in her company. There I was, with my chance alone with her, and guess what, girls? I, your glib, always-in-command Lulu, couldn't say a word. I simply turned to look at her as I left the room, and—are you ready for the full significance of this, dear reader?—*I caught her looking at my ass.*

Yes, she was checking me out. Now we all know that the Lulu-bottom has become less like a set of kiwifruit and more like a couple of overripe melons in the long breakup misery after Elena—a fact we are working hard to remedy, mind you—but Peggy was looking, and not with disgust. She saw me turn and her eyes came to rest on my face. I believe I was grinning idiotically. This tiny bit of endorsement, you may well believe, shot your Lulu straight into the stratosphere, and I still haven't come down. Every time I think of that look, I get that delicious little flutter in the tummy. You know that flutter. It's a lovely flutter. We should all get to have that flutter, all the time.

So now I have to wax the bikini area before I go back to Pilates tomorrow. Because you never quite know who's going to walk into the sauna, do you?

Soon to be follicle-free,

Lu

May 18

Hello my lovelies,

Here's something we all need to warm our hearts after the post-Mother's-Day-nuclear fallout. No, I am not going to bring up once again the tense discussion I continue to have with my mother over the exact nature of Rox and Stacey's relationship. My mother, it seems, has continued to tell herself that Rox and Stacey are some variety of "roommates" or perhaps their partnership has some business associations, but at any rate they are "just friends." Likewise, she sincerely believes of my own various attachments—starting with Debbie and continuing up through Elena—that these, also, were no more than "close" friendships. Somewhat like the "romantic friendships" women were allowed to have in the nineteenth century, which to straight women means they just hugged a lot, while the rest of us know exactly what was going on, or at least can imagine the possibilities.

Meanwhile I have tried again and again to explain to this mother of mine how, why, and in what ways women can be attracted to other women. She still refuses to get it. I beg of you, do not press me to dwell upon the tenor of these discussions, for they raise Lulu's blood pressure and send her running for the emergency chocolate stash (which, by the way, Harvey my editor has discovered and apparently regards as his very own candy store. Men!!).

The last ridiculous thing my mother said to me—and I repeat it only briefly, since I believe I have wrestled with this issue enough times in the past, as a quick glance at the daily posts will suggest—was that she blames my father for this aversion to men. *Aversion,* she calls it. I think I will have to stop speaking to her for a while again. I maintain that I am an adult now and can handle my temper, but I don't see how I can legitimately be asked to refrain from responding with nasty comments when she started it.

So, rather, let me applaud and give the cockles-of-the-heart-warming story of the month award to Tempe Tillie and her description of how she took the opportunity, this Mother's Day, to face her family with the news that, post-retirement, post her sixty-fifth birthday, and almost two decades post her divorce, she has fallen in love: with a woman. Tillie, you and Renate are an inspiration to us all. The way you handled your children was wonderful. I think you have every right to call yourselves the Gleeful Grannies, and you shouldn't be the least shy about a small public display of affection here and there (since I'm assuming it would, of course, be tasteful, and not include going at it on a park bench like bunnies). I will consider it your personal duty to update us on the sex-after-sixty scene.

Imagine living in a world where people assume that menopause eliminates your sex drive! Violence against women reaches everywhere, it seems.

Renewing her subscription to *Bitch* (and you should, too),

Lu-living-out-her-inner-bitch-Lu

May 22

Ah, la vie est belle.

Great girl-time today with Suze, who is my needed antidote to the mother-poison. Suze and I, as you know, are updating our *Guide to Your Inner Lesbian,* though there's been a bit of a tussle at the publisher's since apparently Felice Newman's next edition of *The Whole Lesbian Sex Book* is due for release at that time. (You can afford to support both of these worthy projects, can't you, dear reader?) Apparently Suze is getting mail for William Harkin delivered to her, too, which makes me wonder if the problem is not, after all, said William's irresponsibility with his change-of-address cards but rather some caprice on the part of our mail carrier (the interestingly androgynous one with the hoop in the ear and the uniform which hides his/her completely indiscernible physique, though why I should be preoccupied with slotting her into the his/her category I don't know, since as our trans friends will remind me, glands and chromosomes and other biological apparatus neither a gender nor a person make).

Suze inspired some hilarity upon revealing that, after running into the Wildebeest in the weight room the other day, she ended up spending the early evening helping him hang art. She says he has nice art. (This I don't entirely believe, having had some experience with what males in their mid-to-late-twenties consider art.) She refused to detail the interior of the Wildebeest lair, saying that I was showing a morbid curiosity about it, but she is certain Willy is straight. (I am certain Willy is gay—what straight man knows anything, I repeat, about art?) Suze also issued the final ruling that he is an innocuous dork. I maintain that Willy is a malignant dork, that in his very clueless and non-observantness he perpetuates the prejudices and the behaviors that have led to women being considered second-class citizens for too long. This is the part where Suze queued up the second season of "Queer as Folk" and fixed me another rum Alexander.

And, let me tell you, I needed it. Peggy is clearly not interested in me. She spent the whole hour of Pilates today coaching and correcting the alignment of Vera, the Bavarian beauty who lives down the hall from me. Damn the allure of the accent! I brought Vera because I thought she would be the perfect wing-girl; we have good times, but she is so glaringly straight that I was sure she would create the perfect pseudo-chaperone environment for some chaste and provocative flirting. Instead, Vera's oblivious hetero impulses appear to present an intriguing challenge to Peggy, who as we know has a history of falling for straight girls. While I, oh-so-available Lu, seem to be giving off the desperation vibes. I'll never fall in love again. Elena was the last time I had sex. I'll be alone forever.

Blue,

Lu

May 31

To the ladies of my life,

So the latest love-bomb goes to Rhonda of Rhode Island, for her post about GLSEN and how she took over leadership of her school's local chapter. Kudos to you, Rhonda, for taking a stand against harassment and in favor of education. That's what this column is for: awareness, folks, enough awareness to end the bigotry and the hate. Rhonda, we've put a link to GLSEN's home page on our sidebar of Lulu-approved resources and support networks. No more teens should have to die because of sexual orientation, whether they're practicing lesbians or simply saying they're lesbians to turn off a couple of creepy guys who want to "party."

And to bring some joy back into your life after reading the depressing headlines, check out Lulu's candid article on sex toys in the latest issue of *Girlfriends*. If no one else in the world will love us, we have to work all the harder at loving ourselves.

Lush with lavender,

Lulu

June 5

Good evening, my chickadees.

So you remember my neighbor from down the hall, Willy the Wildebeest? I have a fire safety story to tell you today. Girls and girl-lovers, if you are the type of person who will sleep through a fire alarm, could you please, out of courtesy for your friends and neighbors, turn the smoke detector in your apartment off unless you actually do have a situation where there is a fire?

Let me tell you the story. I'm folding my laundry. Lulu and her laundry. What else does a single no-prospect girl do on a Saturday afternoon? After you recover from those martinis of the previous night and before you make plans to have martinis that evening, there are, as you all know, long stretches of recovery and preparation which are best filled with some productive activity, perhaps a long bath, painting the toenails, cleaning the storage area, what have you. So I am folding my laundry when a fire alarm down the hall starts letting out an awful racket.

Did I suspect immediately it was Willy the Wildebeest? Did I know somehow that this would turn into drama? Yes, ladies and lovelies, I did. Certain young men should never be loosed on the world as single adults but rather *should* live with their mothers until they marry or otherwise acquire a partner who will be able to care for them, perhaps a pretty nurse in the assisted-living manor. (You all remember my story about the pretty nurse at the assisted-living manor? If not go back to the Lulu archives and read

"Getting Old Can't Be All Bad.")

I was folding my delicates, which is a process that requires focused attention, so you can imagine my annoyance at this initial distraction. Then, as the alarm continued and no one attended to it—and there was no indication of smoke—I continued, as you can imagine, to become annoyed. I folded; the alarm clanged. I moved on to my sleepwear; still the alarm. I was getting the folds and creases all wrong, such a state of mind was I in at this moment. Finally I realized that I could no longer rely on the kindness of strangers to attend to their alarm, and I must confront the perpetrator myself. (Besides, as you know, I knew it was William.)

Imagine, if you can, my pique at this moment! Imagine how I seethed! I wonder if you really can imagine. Laundry-folding time is as important as bubble-bath time to me. Lulu is very defensive about her private rituals—as you should be too, dear reader, since our private spaces must be protected, particularly since we the marginalized, we the odd, we the "out," we the women pigeon-holed by society into becoming an identity bound up in sexual preference rather than as a person with emotional and intellectual resources—I digress. To my story: feeling like a heroine gallantly going to confront the villain, I marched out in the hall. (Since Vera my Bavarian beauty will demand to know what I was wearing, I will tell you now: it was not lacy. It was not sheer or see-through or anything that in any way constitutes delicacy. I was wearing my navy blue Penn State sweatpants and my favorite grey Army T-shirt because, honestly, it is so comfortable, and it does such nice things for my breasts, and you know what Lulu always says—if you can combine beauty *and* comfort, you have found a way to thwart consumer America's designs for its women.) Oh, and I was wearing flip-flops. The pink ones that I bought in Costa Rica when I was there with—well, that story will upset me if I bring it up again, so I will send you back to the archives for December of two years ago for *that* spectacular debacle.

Imagine me, now, knocking briskly at the Wildebeest's door. (Hair in a ponytail.) The fire alarm beeps madly. No one answers. I begin to yell Willy's name. Still there is no response. I imagine him passed out on the floor, asphyxiated by smoke. I debate calling the fire department. Yes, I know how excited you straight girls get when a carload of big strapping men wearing flappy fire-proof things drives up in their big wheeled phallus and starts running all over the place messing up your stuff, but as you might suspect, I am not particularly excited by big uniformed men in any capacity. (A truckload of leggy Latina firefighters, well! You can imagine my reception would be much different.)

At the point where I am threatening to knock down Willy's door, I realize that Willy's door is not locked. I thought all these apartments had self-locking doors, but Willy has resorted to that old dorm trick of gumming up the lock so the door doesn't snap shut behind you, preventing you from being caught in the hall in your underwear and bed-head when all of your friends and your R.A. are at class and all of the people you most particularly loathe and despise are in their rooms studying, and you just know every one of them is going to see you and say something cutting before your roommate can come back from class. So yes, I stormed into Willy's apartment. And I said something terribly clever and high-volume, along the lines of, "Why the *hell* haven't you stopped the fire alarm?"

The Wildebeest was fast asleep on his couch. At least he was not snoring. You know how I feel about snoring, male or female varieties. The fire alarm had not woken him. On a desk by the TV sat a pillar candle, still burning but improperly trimmed, so the flame had bored a hole in the side and hot wax leaked all over everything, and you know how annoying and hyper-sensitive these alarms in this building are—my goodness, you can't even fry an egg without the thing twitching its nose at you. So now hot wax has dripped all over the surface of the Willy's desk and from there onto the carpet, and I do not want to be the Willy when he tries to have an exit interview with the management with clumps of yellow wax fused into his beige rug. Since I, like you, am a woman of action, I blew out the candle, and then I grabbed a nearby article to catch the dripping hot wax. I thought at the time that the papers I grabbed were wrestling tickets, but it seemed a fitting sacrifice. For any other sports admission tickets, of course, I would let Willy's whole apartment go up in flames, but by now you know how I feel about pro wrestling.

During all of this Willy, it seemed, had no idea that the fire alarm was going off (until I stopped that via the usual means), his candle was burning out of control, or his front door was wide open and someone was inside of his apartment. I marched over to him and repeated my question in his ear, at no lesser volume. He actually didn't move until I prodded him in the arm.

This is the point where readers of any other column would be quite excited: girl alone with man in drama situation in apartment, girl wearing thong underwear, man not dressed. No, Willy does not sleep in the buff; Willy is neither a boxer man nor a brief man but prefers boxer briefs, or at least owns a set of the Calvin Klein variety which he was wearing at the time. Willy—and I observe this with an entirely detached eye—could perhaps work as a Calvin Klein model, if he gets fired from his day job, whatever his day job is. As I poked him in the shoulder (nicely muscled, neither hard nor flabby) it occurred to me that Vera, my beautiful Bavarian friend down the hall, would very much like to be in my place at this moment. However, it had clearly fallen to me to save J building from total immolation.

He came awake instantly. That's the funniest moment in all this.

He looked at me and said, "Lulu? What are you doing with my wrestling tickets?"

He was not happy when I explained the situation. He believed I should not have used his tickets to the Apeman-meets-Projectile Boy match to gather dripping hot wax. I reminded him that he should never have gone to sleep with a candle burning without properly trimming the wick. I don't believe he had ever heard about trimming the wick. It was a scented candle, pineapple I think—not the highest-grade pineapple wax you will ever smell. I explained this to him too. Additionally, I pointed out that, as a public service, people should not sleep through fire alarms.

He told me that Nyquil makes him sleep through everything: alarms, telephone, babies crying. (I hope he tells his future wife this before she decides to procreate with him.) He did look somewhat feverish. This still gave him no right to yell at me, though I had every right to yell at him, which of course I was doing.

He stopped yelling when I demonstrated that the cool wax peeled right off the paper as well as the desk. He's on his own about the carpet. I also told him he should lock his door.

"Why?" he said. "What if somebody needs to get in here?"

I had no response to that. I suppose if one has a set of wrestling tickets which one considers valuable but one is also the type of person to leave one's door unlocked, one is on one's own to deal with the possible repercussions or contradictions of that.

"I'm going to finish folding my laundry now," I told Willy firmly. "Let's make sure this never happens again."

You know, girls—straight girls, you can listen in here—I always thought that somebody took a grease pen to the proofs and drew those ab muscles on the underwear models, but Willy has a real sixpack. Apparently he thought I was examining his undergarments, because he said, snapping the elastic waistband, "Very comfortable, no chafing. Try them and you never go back."

Sounds like me and my discovery of the thong.

Now remember how I've always been extraordinarily curious about the inside of the Wildebeest's apartment? And how I imagined it a perfect Cro-Magnon cave, complete with bones on the floor? I may have been a wee bit mistaken. He has a Williams Sonoma set of cooking pots, matched stainless steel, and he has a cutting board and knife rack from the Pampered Chef. He has a series of nicely framed Ansel Adams prints and makes himself lapsang souchong tea when he has a congested head. In my opinion, he still teeters dangerously on the borderline of malignant dork status. I was glad, though, that this conversation wasn't taking place inside of my apartment, with laundry scattered over every surface, a pile of dishes in the sink, possibly a layer of dust on the TV. Willy even has plants. Plants!

Perhaps I will ask him to recommend a plant species, now that I've decided to make the big step of adoption. Perhaps he can give me some tips on plant care.

Once back to my own apartment, hanging my hand-washed brassieres up to dry, I realized I should have peeked into Willy's bedroom, for Vera's sake. If Vera truly is attached to the idea of dating William, perhaps I will arrange for him to cook her spaghetti in his Williams Sonoma cookware and steep her lapsang souchong tea. When he brings out the scented candle and suggests they spend the evening playing backgammon, that is when she will realize that Suze was wrong and I, of course, was right.

The question that consumes me now is: are boxer briefs really as comfortable as Willy says? If I wear them to the gym, for example, will they help me to pick up girls? All you dykes out there who have tried it, post the site and let me know. We have a duty to inform each other on how we may best free our inner femininity in the service of comfort and looking great.

Love,

Lulu for Fire Marshal

June 9

To Alabama Alice:

Your friend is a fag hag and it's time to do a full-scale intervention. She has to be eased into the knowledge that growing body hair will not catch her a bear. I recommend you follow the advice in *Lulu's Guide to Lavender Living*, which you can buy online for $14.75, plus shipping and handling. Flip to Chapter 4, "When Straight People Get Queer: Handling Fetishes in Your Friends." But remember, be gentle. Just because we do not understand the allure of the penis does not mean it is not a dangerous and powerful thing.

I know I've been a little testy the last couple of days, girls, but I beg you to have patience with me. Elena and I called a détente on our no-speaking war only to devolve into a really bitter session of accusation-slinging and name-calling. She had the nerve—the outrageous nerve!—to call me selfish and self-absorbed and say that I never made her feel loved. Me! At least, as I pointed out to her, I wasn't CHEATING on anybody. At this point she slammed out of the café, leaving me with the knowledge that she will never return *Everybody Says I Love You* and I will have to go out, once again, and replace my copy. I tell you, some days it seems like romantic relationships do nothing but deplete your video collection, your youthful optimism, and your lingerie drawer, since you have to throw away the things that acquire too painful of associations, don't you know.

Time to take the inner lesbian out to play. Love,

Lulu, the Best Girlfriend You'll Never Have

June 11

So, the counts are in and the votes have been tallied, and the results are these:

Famous Actress We'd Most Want for Friend-Friend: Ellen de Generes

Famous Actress We'd Most Want for Domestic Partner: Jodie Foster (though, if in fact the suppositions are untrue and Jodie Foster is *not* a lesbian, we all hereby apologize profusely)

Famous Actress We Most Want to Sleep With: Angelina Jolie

Famous Actress Even Straight Girls Would Turn For: Angelina Jolie

Our Angelina also steals the most votes in the categories of Best Lips, Best Butt, and Best Boobs, though I suspect that many voters cast repeat ballots and thus may have tipped the scales overmuch. Nonetheless, I am all too content to acknowledge Angelina as the reigning queen.

And, although this category was much more contested, Favorite Character on The L-Word: Shane.

Still taking votes for Best Screen Kiss in Recent Movie, so visit Lulu's message board and add your voice to the melee.

Hearts to you,

Lulu

June 12

Sisters,

I am in serious trouble. Tonight I finally had a date with Peggy.

As dates go, this one ranks quite high on the Fun and Titillating Scale. We played ping pong, drove bumper cars, ate cotton candy. Arms brushed. Fingers brushed. Then shoulders brushed. I thought sure that would send me straight into raptures. It did not. I gathered that she was sending me a strong signal when she smeared the cotton candy on my cheek and then licked it off. (Have you ever had someone smear cotton candy on your face and then lick it off? Try it sometime.) I could have grabbed her right then. But as she was driving us back to her place, where I'd left my car, I knew. I did not want to sleep with her. I did not want to touch her. I did not want to lick any part of her body. I did not even want to kiss her.

After all the Pilates classes, all the longing, all the mournful looks. What is the *matter* with me?

What do you do when you're with somebody and intellectually and rationally you can appreciate her with complete sincerity, can admit to yourself that she fulfills all your aesthetic requirements, would even go so far as to say that by anyone's standards she is a knockout, is a brilliant and wonderful and fantastic and perfect human being, but you *just don't want to have sex with her?*

I can tell you what Lulu did, and it was pretty ugly. I stammered something ridiculous when we got to her place and hopped in my car as soon as possible. All the way home I felt sorry for myself and, consequently, played Amy and Emily as loud as I could—switching between "Galileo" and "Closer to Fine," Lulu's favorites. I suppose I'll have to send Peggy flowers or something to apologize. She'll think it's something she did, when it's just me.

And of course, now I have to quit the gym. What with all the chocolate it is going to take to deal with this fiasco, plus the time lost in finding a new gym, I can expect to gain at least five if not seven pounds due to Peggy fallout. I suppose I could start using the weight room in my apartment building, but weirdos like Willy the Wildebeest hang out there.

I came home in such a stew that not even the Love Handler could help me sort this mess out. (For all who don't know, the Love Handler is my vibrator—look back at mid-March of last year . . . actually, it could be February . . . all right, I think the Love Handler played a big part of that long cruel darkest part of winter, so if you look anywhere in those months you'll be sure to run across a mention.) Any way I look at it, I figure there has got to be something wrong with me. The Love Handler says the physical parts are working fine, so it must be something in the mental parts that needs a little oil, a little repair.

I don't need another sex toy, I need a shrink. In the meantime, I will be single forever.

Yours in eternal celibacy,

Lulu the Most Wretched

June 17

Okay ladies,

The thread is getting out of hand, so I'm going to make a final pronouncement on Nasty Nanette and her dilemma. Nan, girl, go ahead with your little testosterone experiment if you're determined to do so, but I warn you that he only wants to add you to the Brag List. I agree that we shouldn't let the labels define us, who cares if it's bisexual or questioning or something else altogether, love is love is love, the heart wants what it wants, and so on and so on and so forth. But everything you've said about this guy, sister, makes it sounds like he's just out to bag a "lesbian chick" so he can boast to his buddies about his overwhelming masculinity. If you're fine with being some gorilla's conversion anecdote, that's up to you, but please make sure there are several layers of latex between his nasty bits and yours.

And speaking of nasty bits, do post the after-coitus ratings for us: how big the package, how long till lift-off, and what he screams in the primal moment. I'm sure our boy-loving readers will get a kick out of that. And when you return to your senses and come back to the light, we will require no more than a full-body immersion in chlorinated water to wash away the effects of your temporary madness.

Air kisses for you but not your hairy friend,

Lulu (who is due for a Brazilian wax herself, come to think of it)

P.S. Thanks to Manhattan Mandy for her post-Peggy encouragement, and for her report on her sticky cotton-candy night with her own sex kitten. Montana Marge, you cracked me up completely—that's exactly how you feel about your husband, indeed! If marriage is the death of sex, we're better off calling it a commitment ceremony and keeping the U-Haul number programmed into the cell phone. And the heart-warming-story-of-the-month award goes, this time, to Sally from Sarasota; so brave, and only fourteen! Thanks for your honesty, girl, and for proving that not all mothers are intolerant and unreasonable.

June 21

Hey there babes and dolls,

Check this out. Lulu went out last night. Yes, actually set foot outside of her apartment, on a weeknight, to a place that was not a bar (well actually we did go to a bar but that was later) and not a dance club. I went to a sporting event. I know! How totally crazy, right?

Here's how it happened. It was all due to Willy. Yes, my neighbor the Wildebeest, who continues to open new horizons for little Lulu. Of course you must remember we use this word loosely when we apply it to me—I am all of 6'0" in my slippered feet. But Willy is 6'4"—the uncomfortable recollections of Elena's infidelity associated with this measurement are becoming less and less painful, thank goodness—so I don't exactly tower over him.

I'd decided to devote the night to maintenance, which every girl has to do once in a while. After a hot bath, a facial mask, a loofah scrub, and a thorough waxing job, I'd gotten to the toenail painting and the hot oil treatment for the hair about the time the knock came on my door. Fortunately my second coat of Hot Mama Scarlet Satin Finish was well on its way to drying, so I waddled to the door, taking care not to dislodge the little toe spacers with the smiley faces on them.

Now, it does not bother me to open the door in my bathrobe with a damp towel wrapped around my head, and it should not embarrass you either, dear reader. You must imagine that my face would be attractively flushed from the bath and scrub, my legs were freshly shaven, and besides it is a plush white Victoria's Secret bathrobe, about mid-thigh, with the monogrammed letters. Additionally I hoped my caller was either Vera or perhaps the receptionist from the management office, whom I am pretty sure is straight, but you never know.

But no, it was Willy standing there. He looked a little embarrassed. More embarrassed, at any rate, than I was. He was fully dressed, in a blue button-down shirt which managed not to look too stuffy because he was also wearing jeans. He held two slips of paper in his hand.

"I have tickets to the Twins game tonight," he said. "And no one to go with."

"Cool, I'll take them," I said, and made a grab for the little slips of paper. I knew I could call on any number of girls who would be my date.

He moved his hand. "But I want to go. I just haven't found anyone who wants the second ticket."

"That's okay, I'll take it," I said. "How much do I owe you?"

"What I mean is, I want somebody to go with me," he said.

I eyed him doubtfully. (You'll think I'm making this conversation up, but I render it exactly.) I said, "How about you just give me the ticket?"

"Well, you can take it, but you'd still have to sit next to me," he said. "So we might as well show up together."

He had a point there.

"How long do I have to get ready?" I asked.

He looked at the towel, then at the toe spacers. He observed, I am sure, the little smiley faces. "What, you're not ready now? Just like that?"

"I'm sure the team would adore the bathrobe," I said. "But I might get a little chilly."

"The game starts at eight."

Lulu did some quick mental math: ten minutes to buy beers and find our seats, thirty minutes to get across town in a cab, but I still had to blow dry my hair, put on the top coat over the Hot Mama Scarlet Satin Finish, and decide what lipstick I wanted to wear. "Give me twenty minutes," I said, deciding to be optimistic.

"All right," he said. (A witty conversation, no?) I turned and headed back to the bathroom, my spirits lifting at the thought of meeting some awesome big-shouldered butch girls at the game.

At this point, I realized that when I headed back to the bathroom, Willy stepped into my apartment. He looked around him. He came into my living room and sat down. Then he stood up and wandered around. I looked pointedly at him. He looked at my artwork.

"You don't plan to wait here, do you?"

He seemed surprised by this. "Why not?"

"But you'll look at things."

"Yeah," he said, "starting with your underwear drawer."

"I don't want you *looking* at my things. They're *my* things."

"I'm not going to touch anything." He sat down on The Magic Couch and put his hands on his knees. If you could have seen him, dear reader, you'd have laughed. The Magic Couch, as you know, is pretty big, but a 6'4" man can manage to make just about any piece of furniture look undersized.

"I don't believe you," I said.

"Look, will you just get ready? You could have been dressed in the time you've stood here arguing with me."

When I came out of the bedroom in my favorite jeans and a cute tight tee, the blue one that says "princess" on it, Willy was stretched out on the couch with his feet up on the glass coffee table reading my copy of *The Bell Jar*. "I haven't read this since high school," he said. "I totally forgot how awesome Plath is."

I wasn't assigned *The Bell Jar* until college. I wonder what kind of high school Willy went to. I'll bet he was the nerd in Advanced Lit.

About five minutes after we found our seats sat down with our beers, I realized that if I hadn't actually wanted to see the game, I could have made some real money by raffling off Willy's extra ticket to any one of the half dozen women eyeing him up. He was getting some pretty serious studies. I suppose he's good-looking, as men go. He's got all that dark curly hair and there's nothing wrong with his face. I will say this for him: he has nice lips. It's important that a man have nice lips.

When I pointed out all the girls who were looking at him, he said, "Would you stop looking at all of the women?"

"Are you uncomfortable to be here with your neighbor the lesbian?" I challenged him. "Are you feeling threatened by my sexuality?" I believe I may have raised my voice a little bit. I believe the people a few rows behind us may have heard.

"I'm not going to get into a contest with you about who can pick up more chicks," he said.

I told him I had no intention of starting such a silly contest. Because, of course, I'd lose. Lulu the infinitely untouched is not going to get any action.

Especially at a ball game. Though, considering that all of the girls I saw were with boyfriends, Willy wouldn't have much of a chance either. But still a better chance than I had, I don't doubt.

As it turns out, the game was great—the Twins won, go team!—and we went out for a drink afterwards and ran into the group that had been sitting right behind us, and they joined our table and we ate their chicken wings and it was a pretty good time all around. Willy borrowed my copy of *The Bell Jar* because he said he lost a box of books in the move, and when I told him I wanted advice on houseplant care he took me into his apartment and had me choose a spider plant and made a cutting right there. He said you can't kill a spider plant, even if you're trying. He put the cutting in a glass of water (glass, not plastic—I don't think Willy even owns any plastic utensils) and told me to let it grow a root and then let him know and he'd help me pot it. I'm not quite sure about how I feel about setting up a situation where I must rely on Willy to get me started in houseplant care. His plants seem to be thriving, however, so it's just as good as asking the guy at the nursery. Better, in fact, because I can bang on Willy's door any time to ask for help if my plant is ailing—as long as he's not sleeping, ha ha.

Well, girls, it's time to go to espn.com and see if I'm in any of the crowd shots from last night's game. I guess Willy the Wildebeest isn't so bad. Unfortunately it doesn't seem that he knows any beautiful, exciting women he can set me up with. Willy doesn't trigger the gaydar, but neither do I see beautiful and exciting women trooping in and out of his apartment. Maybe he's a confirmed bachelor. Or maybe he's asexual. Not that I care either way; I get an eyeful of hetero sex every time I flip through the cable stations, so I don't need a guy friend who wants to make me privy to his exploits. But a friend I can take to sporting events who won't bother me a bit if he runs off with a 6'4" guard, now that is something I can use in my life.

Here's your Lulu signing off, and reminding you to give that little girl inside you some candy every once in a while.

June 26

Ladies, I'm excited about this houseplant. The adoption is official. Willy and I potted the Sprout and it's a real plant now. Willy made fun of the container I picked out, but we already know about Willy's tastes. I put Sprout in the window and he seemed to like it fine. This is what you get when you take a plant cutting from your straight male neighbor: a straight male plant. Yes, Willy is straight. My gaydar might need a little tuning, but these vibes read loud and clear. I just hope the crushing disappointment of discovering he doesn't know any literary lesbians will be lessened by the companionship of my new pet. I suppose I'll have to get used to a male presence. At least he doesn't make much of a mess.

Of course, about the time I'm telling Rox and Stacey about my new addition, they've got news of their own: they've decided to have a *baby*. Whoa, I say. This is a serious, serious commitment. Sleepless nights. Stinky diapers. A constant drain on your finances, starting with the truly terrifying array of toys and other products aimed at infants and then moving on to cars and college.

You should have seen, dear reader, the gleams in their respective eyes as they held hands on their couch and explained that Rox was going to be the baby mommy. Stacey's afraid the hormone imbalance might screw up her work on her dissertation, and Rox can keep doing massage right up to the moment she delivers, more or less. They wanted me to help pick out the baby daddy from the profiles they got from the donor center. (Thank goodness they're not doing it the old-fashioned way—too much ick.) It seems they'd pretty much decided to favor the astrophysicist from MIT, the one employed by NASA, though I personally thought they should choose the Irish musician and see if they couldn't hit on a red-haired and blue-eyed combo, given our family's recessive genes.

A baby. I'm still trying to take this in. It's such a big step for us. Good thing I've adopted a plant for practice, because the little offshoot is going to need plenty of love and guidance and spoiling from her Aunty Lu. Though I suppose this means I won't be Rox and Stacey's chief darling anymore. I'm being replaced.

A bit overwhelmed, but on the whole pleased with her new responsibilities,

Lu

P.S. Peggy resigned from the gym. I feel curiously unguilty about this. It can't entirely be my fault, and probably has more to do with the fact that her ex and the ex's newly reacquired husband are moving back to town than with the fact that I've removed my gaze-worthy bottom from the Pilates class. As a matter of fact, I feel relieved. Now I can sign up for the evening yoga class and see if that Australian swimmer still does seven o'clock laps...

P.P.S. Elena's basketball guard left her. That's where karma gets you, folks. Elena called me last night and, when I didn't answer, left a five-minute-long sobbing message. I wanted to call her back but I couldn't—I just couldn't. I know it would be the big-hearted thing to do, but really . . . do I have to be that big-hearted, to help out the ex who dumped ME by listening to her heart break over being dumped by the woman she left me for? Guess I still have some growing up to do. But as I figure, I've got nine months, maybe more, to get my head in the game. I can do this.

July 1

To Kinky Kate and all you brown baggers out there:

What is this crap? Buying your toys online and waiting for them to come wrapped in nondescript brown paper? What are you, ashamed of yourself? Ladies, have a little pride. Grab your gal (or a couple of gal pals – if you have more than one gal without an understanding you are a CHEATER and you know how I feel about THAT) and take her to the nearest feminine-friendly bookstore/toy shop and coo over the possibilities together. What better way to bond? Believe me, girls, the couple that plays together, stays together. There is no need any longer for us to go skulking about the corners of adult stores as though we were doing something wrong. Slap on that nametag that says "Hi, my name is Muff Diver" and stick out your chest. There's precious little love in the world. Additionally, if you have any opportunity whatsoever for grand sex, you should leap at it.

And to Tex and all the rest of you who are getting your male hormones fired up over my perfectly bland and non-charged and not-going-anywhere just-hanging-out-a-couple-of-nights-a-week with Willy: back off, buckaroo. And read the archives. Once you know about Frosh Doug (fornicator, beer-bong-buster, and multiple-infidelity-performer—yes, Doug, the entire cheerleading team counts INDIVIDUALLY) and Debbie, my college love who introduced me to screwdrivers, the Indigo Girls, and the pleasures of female companionship—not to mention Randi, Libby, and that intoxicating Charity or whatever her name was who I met in Costa Rica–well, I don't think you'll have reason to doubt me. Clearly there were some boys in the unenlightened days of my conflicted and anxiety-ridden youth, but I'm a girl-lover at heart.

And if you don't believe me, call Suze and she'll confirm it. Or better yet, call Vera. She's desperate for dates.

Love to all of you (though you're toeing a dangerous line, Texas),

Lu

P.S. Nanette, you can stop anytime now with telling us the disgusting details of your ongoing gorilla affair. This is a lavender website, if you please. Start a blog if you really do have to discuss, at length, the way he yells "oh shit" when he's climaxing. If/when you return to your senses or have an interesting threesome, you can come back.

July 3

My stars,

It's so irritating when your queer romance horoscope tells you that the sparks are about to fly between you and the one you've had your eye on. Hello, aren't you people supposed to be psychic? Can't you see that I am—perhaps permanently—in the landscape of loneliness and rejection? Elena is starting to cyberstalk me, posting endless pictures of little girls cuddling kittens to my Facebook timeline. It's not like she wants ME back, she just wants someone to listen to her. There are paid professionals to do that. Meantime, I sit at home, change my pedicure polish, read the latest selection of my Lesbian Reading Circle, and try to decide if Sprout is getting enough water. Enough thrill to kill a normal person, not to mention your little Lulu.

Of course, Suze and I have plans to go watch the fireworks tomorrow, so there's always a chance that a spark will fall on one of us and then there will be a fire, just like the horoscope says.

Yours and grumpy,

Spark free (but still sparkly), Lu

July 7

Guess what.

Willy couldn't find me last night (at the gym—toning those flabby deltoids) so he took Vera the over-bosomed Bavarian to the basketball game. I'm sure she drooled on him the entire time. Bitches. The Australian swimmer wasn't even in the pool, and now I have to turn on ESPN to see how the Twins did.

July 11

Okay guys and dolls,

I know I've been a little bit obsessed with the personal side of things lately, but we must not forget that the whole purpose of LuluThe Lesbian.com is awareness, with a touch of activism when needed, and right now your Lulu is suffering a keen consciousness-raising (or maybe conscience-raising) experience. What am I talking about? Breast cancer. It's not just a punishment for straight girls. Did you know that over two hundred *thousand* new cases of breast cancer will be diagnosed this year? And that's in the U.S. alone, not even including our sisters abroad. It's the leading cause of death for American women between ages 40 and 55, even more than heart disease. Did you know that every 12 minutes, an American woman dies of breast cancer? That's the time it takes to catch up on Lulu's latest posts, even if your double caramel macchiato is slowing you down.

And breast cancer doesn't affect just women. Men get it too.

How did my so-sensitive heart get prickled, you might ask? Willy showed up at my door (I forget why—we had made plans for something, or maybe he was just checking on Sprout) wearing a white T-shirt with a little pink ribbon affixed to it. I'm ashamed to say I kidded him about it. He said he was advertising National Mammography Day, coming up in October. I didn't even know they still did mammograms; I thought for sure the technology had to have evolved by now. Apparently drug researchers are pouring their money into the latest anti-impotency drug for men and still don't give a damn for women's diseases. The violence is everywhere, I tell you.

Anyway, it turns out Willy's mom is a breast cancer survivor, or close to. She's been in remission for six years, but now there's growth in the other breast. She might have to get that one removed, too. One more reason to be thankful I'm a small-breasted woman, I guess; less room for tumors to take root. Of course I didn't say that to Willy. I do have *some* sensitivity.

Turns out—I don't know quite how it happened—I'm signed up on Willy's team to run the Relay for Life at the local high school at the end of the month. We get people to pledge money, we walk 25 miles in circles around this track, and that is supposed to make life easier for people with breast cancer.

Think I can do it? How much do you love me? Enough to make a donation—enough that I can bring in more pledges than Willy? You believe in your Lulu, don't you? You know she's a faithful member of Curves? Just go to https://www.gotthat.com/helpluluwintherelayforlife, where you can pay with your handy credit card, and together we will give research funding for women's health issues a good swift kick in the you-know-what.

Love & kisses,

Lupe Lu

July 13

Rita in Ravensdale, you are not alone. Here's a whammy-sized Lulu-love-bomb coming right at you. You remind us of something it's easy to forget; religion doesn't leave a lot of room for the lesbian, gay, trans, bi, or questioning among us. I've added a bunch of links to the sidebar; you, Rita my dove, might want to look at catholiclesbians.org. I've checked out a couple of meetings of the group in my town (I admit, I was not just craving spiritual guidance, but also meeting like-minded people—maybe single, seeking ones, too). If you're among the right people—people who want to create a warm and loving environment, that is, and are concerned with more than just bitching about their personal problems—it can be a really transformative event. Besides, once your spiritual life is on track—and this should serve as a reminder for all of us that the spiritual life needs to come *first*—this could be a great way to meet fit, sympathetic, great-looking girls. Because we have bodies that need nourishment too, you know. (Though Lulu herself is turning into a starving wolf—but we won't talk about that right now.) Although you remind me, the Unitarian church has changed its services to a more reasonable hour on Sunday mornings . . .

Looking to get her halo polished,

Lu

P.S. Don't forget to make your pledges for my Relay for Life team! Don't let Willy get pledged more money than I do! If you can't do it for me, do it for Willy's mom!!

July 15

Tex & company,

Back OFF, man. The sparks are not flying with anyone, much less Willy, who is as much a Wildebeest is ever. Imagine—he criticizes the "The L-Word" by saying it's unrealistic that all the women have the same body type and he thinks it mostly caters to male erotic fantasies. The nerve of him! It is just a TV show, Willy—it is not meant to resemble life! It is one thing for me to make a well-founded assessment about the shape of supermodels but quite another for Willy not to have a sense of humor about a show that is designed to be entertaining. Men really do not get it sometimes.

But, in case Tex or any of the rest of you needs a reminder, let me say again: Sprout is the only male in my world, the sole light of my dark and celibate life. Just because you, Tex, regularly get laid by your redneck buddies' ho-bag girlfriends doesn't mean the rest of us must sink to your undiscriminating standards. The column reads Lulu the LESBIAN and if you don't know what that word means maybe you should have someone read the entry to you from the dictionary. Or better yet, have the buddies' girlfriends demonstrate. Might teach you a thing or two about improving your own technique, pal.

July 19

So, chiclets,

Rox and Stacey have made their decision and scheduled their big Implantation Day. I'll go with them to act as hand-holder and driver, since they're both so nervous and giddy already that it's doubtful either one of them will have the sense to get to the clinic and back. Rox has been informed that some women experience nausea after the procedure, and Stacey always vomits when she's excited or upset.

But I get to design invitations and favors for the Post-Implantation party, which I'm looking forward to. We're going to have grape-juice mimosas and I'm going to make little peach-and-lace pouches that I'll fill with candy hearts. It's the only thing I could think of to remotely invoke an egg in the uterus but still be tasteful.

Also, I'm going to tell guests to choose their gifts from A Pea in the Pod—maternity wear doesn't have to be ugly any longer! I almost wish I could be pregnant, just to wear some of those cute clothes. Though, of course, the idea of some alien consciousness invading my body and appropriating my internal organs is enough to make me content to admire the maternity wear from afar.

Willy happened to be over when Rox and Stacey stopped by to tell me the big news. We'd planned to go hiking that day—Willy is a big outdoors freak as you know, but since it was storming we decided to have a *Matrix* marathon instead so we could both drool over Carrie Ann Moss and I could covertly ogle Keanu Reeves, whose androgyny, I must admit, I find titillating. To my surprise, Willy seemed to hit it off with Rox and Stacey, though they are normally so discriminating and are very effective at repelling dorks.

Willy got a little annoying when he started talking about how his sister's baby is now two so they're probably ready to get rid of some furniture and stuff so maybe Rox and Stacey would want to take a look, and they were nice enough to seem pleased and flattered even though I know they've been looking at new nursery sets and they definitely don't want anything that's been beaten up, chewed on, or recalled. They even went so far—too far, in my opinion—as to invite Willy to the Post-Implantation party, an idea I will be hasty to discourage, if he brings it up again, since I know Rox and Stacey have some really hot, sophisticated friends I haven't met yet, and I definitely won't get hit on at their party if I bring Willy as my date. So far Willy and I haven't had to compete for women, but I wouldn't want to start.

He'd get points with a straight woman for how much he loves kids, though; he certainly was quick to bring out pictures of his niece, and it's clear he adores her. I'm sure I'll have plenty of baby-sitting duties starting nine months from now, so maybe Willy can give me some pointers on how to entertain a tiny drooling human entity.

And if I ever did decide to take on such a reckless and enormous responsibility, it's possible Willy wouldn't be so awful a pick for a baby daddy. He has a good job, he has no genetic deformities that I've yet seen, and as weird as he may be at times, he was completely cool with Rox and Stacey, so he has nothing against lesbian couples. But that sort of thing never seems to work out in the movies, and I'd be wary of trying it in real life.

Time to go sew the little peach pouches.

Lovingly,

Lu

P.S. A big hearty thanks to all who have pledged—I love, adore, am awash with infatuation for you! For those who haven't pledged yet: as the dollar drops in value every moment, I urge you to pledge *now* to get the most bang for your buck. Willy has a city baseball league that I just found out he plays for, and he's been shameless about begging them for money. Don't let your Lulu down!

July 26

My darlings,

Lulu learned something about herself today. She learned that she, also, has a tendency to vomit when she's nervous or upset. Must be a family tic.

There I was, in my bathroom and in great distress, no less than twenty minutes before I was supposed to pick up Rox and Stacey for our ceremonial Implantation, and not only could I not get ahold of Suze but Vera wasn't answering her door, either, and dear oh dear, what was a girl to do? I couldn't go to the management office to ask for help and let the pretty receptionist see me like this, even though an engagement ring has recently appeared on her finger (drat and double-drat).

And who, then, should stroll through my door—finding me in the bathroom, very green around the gills—but Willy, calm and unconcerned and as casual as could be in his T-shirt and Birkenstocks and battered jeans, with his curly hair uncombed and his face freshly shaven. He'd forgotten it was Implantation Day and he wanted to go to brunch at the new vegan bagel shop, or something equally ridiculous, but I will say this for Willy: he saved us all by driving me to Rox and Stacey's to pick them up, and then he waited in the reception area reading parenting magazines while the three of us trooped into the procedure room, and he even, after dropping us at Rox and Stacey's, ran back to our building to get the party favors and my gifts for each of them, which I in my illness had left behind. After that, of course, I couldn't very well ask him to leave the party.

The peach pouches were a big hit, I must say; Rox laughed so hard that tears came to her eyes when she discovered that, after running out of candy hearts, I had supplemented the lack with Blow-pops. She thought it was meant as a phallic symbol. As if! At least I had brought a bottle of champagne for those of us who weren't pregnant, so a little bubbly took the edge off my humiliation, and helped to settle my stomach, too.

There were plenty of sophisticated women at the party, of course, but no one particularly thrilling. A couple of the straight ones approached Willy—apparently mid-thirties girls don't automatically exclude mid-twenties men from the dating pool anymore—but I see now why Willy is single; he was very clearly giving off the "polite-but-not-interested" vibes. Maybe he is asexual. He doesn't talk about other women, I've noticed. And he spent most of the party helping me mix mimosas and replenish the finger food platters when he could have been circulating, so that tells you

119

something either about his confidence or his technique.

But Rox and Stacey are crazy about him, have pledged an equal amount of money in both our names for our Relay for Life team, and have made arrangements, post-Relay, for all four of us to go to Willy's sister's and take a look at the baby accoutrements he mentioned the other day. I guess I can try to be gracious about their infatuation, as inexplicable as it may seem. I owe Willy big for bailing me out today.

Rox and Stacey really are so ridiculously happy. It's almost depressing. I know it can't be true that certain people suck all the happiness to themselves and don't leave enough to go around for the rest of us, but you have to wonder sometimes—it's like they give off their own light. Enough to make a lump come to girl's throat every now and then. People really can be that crazy in love. People really can make each other that happy.

Getting bigger-hearted all the time (she hopes),

Your Lu

July 27

Note to Tex and the other trash-talkers:

Your asshole-osity is getting rather tiresome. Did you guys miss the millennium or what? These are not the *When Harry Met Sally* days any longer; men and women *can* be friends. You might spend more of your energy trying to locate cute, fun lesbians you can direct to my column as potential dating fare and spend less energy harboring these unkind suspicions about my starting to "swing back the other way," as you put it.

Are you ready to emerge yet from the tyranny of the Y chromosome, or are you really so far back in the cave that you believe everything, still and always, is about getting sex? What are we to make of those compatriots to whom you refer to as friends, then? What am I to think about poker night, or soccer games, or your evenings "hanging out at the bar?" Are you and your buddies just spending that time in the bathroom going at it like rabbits, if everything really is about "getting it on," in your oh-so-eloquent phrase?

Steaming her pores open,

Lu

July 31

Wow.

I don't even know how to talk about this.

In fact, I'm not even sure what the hell happened.

Yes, I went to the Relay for Life. I met Willy's mom and I couldn't stop trying not to stare at her chest. She wasn't wearing her falsie—I guess if there's one place you don't have to strap on your boob, it's for a rally of cancer survivors—so there was a little asymmetry to the "Hosted by Bill's Dairy Bar" T-shirt. I tried not to stare, knowing that breast was being eaten away on the inside too. My own rack hurt, not in sympathy but in fear that the same thing could happen to me. I thought I was going to be sick and I thought there was no way I was going to be able to walk 25 miles. Especially with the smell of grilling hot dogs permeating the air around me.

It was like camp, boys and girls. The camp you used to go to when you were seven, played now by your adult neighbors. There were tents. Willy's mom had a big one. I had a sleeping bag in the back of Willy's car (from that long-ago trip to Costa Rica, and girl did I wish I were back there) and Willy brought one of those chaise lawn chairs that unfolds back and front (or sandwiches you in the middle if you're not careful). He set that up outside his mom's tent and I tossed down my sleeping bag and got introduced to a blur of names and faces (have I mentioned that I'm bad with names *and* faces?) and grimly decided that if Willy's mom could survive weeks of radiation, I could survive one evening of being around slightly freaky, overly warm and enthusiastic, really emotional people.

I managed to miss the opening session and the first march around the track by survivors. I was inside the high school throwing up in the girl's bathroom, and I hadn't even had a hot dog. All I'd eaten were carrots. I figured that would make my night vision fairly sharp for navigating around the track around 3:00 in the morning. We signed up for shifts—there was some chart that the chief of our team, a really big and loud woman with no breasts at all, had filled out with excruciating detail—in glow-in-the-dark pen—and taped to one of the tent posts. But since I didn't remember who anyone was, I wouldn't know who to report to when my shift was done. I saw myself getting stuck in an endless loop all night, walking until the rubber soles burned off my shoes and my knees gave out and I collapsed with exhaustion with my face in the pebbled dirt.

Things improved once the volleyball began. If you know your Lulu, you know she is excellent at volleyball. We won every game. Willy grabbed me and hugged me after every great shot, which got a little embarrassing, because his mom was watching. I think he was starting to catch the overload-on-emotion vibe that was going around.

People kept cheering and crying for about the first ten laps, and then they all settled down and realized it was going to be a long, boring night. Except for the rock stars who were playing volleyball. We won the championship game, thank you very much. We got newer and improved T-shirts for this. Willy stood with his arm around me for all the pictures. At first I thought he was trying to be nice because I was nervous as hell. But having driven the point-winning spike into the face of the snotty girl across from me—who, by the way, would never have been looked at twice in a dyke bar—I was no longer nervous as hell, so there was no reason for the arm. I wondered if Willy was nervous, being surrounded by what were essentially ravaged women and their long-suffering partners and mates.

Then I wondered if he was trying to tell me something. Everyone on our team, and probably all the people camping around us, thought I was Willy's girlfriend. I wondered if I should write something on my shirt. "Lesbian. Available. Small/no breasts a turn-on."

Willy's mom grilled garden burgers and gave me extra tomatoes, which is what made me first start to fall in love with her. I know it's such a cliché to say that people who have escaped death have a great sense of humor and compassion, but this woman is awesome. I had a feeling that I could tell her anything, even the worst and ugliest bits about me, and she would just smile all the way up to her soft brown eyes and then hug me. Willy has his mom's eyes, her eyelashes, her sense of humor. Neither of them mentioned Willy's dad. I wondered if Willy's mom would be willing to adopt me. My mom knows all the worst and ugly parts of me, too, and regularly brings them to my attention.

The people who wanted to sleep through the night took the early evening and late morning shifts, so Willy and I had some time. We didn't know anyone else. Most everyone around us was older, or the infant children of the older people. We went to the playground. Willy pushed me on the swings. I pushed him off the slide. We rode the merry-go-round and I didn't get sick. We talked about our girlfriends. Turns out I have slept with a lot more women than Willy has. He tends to get in serious, long-term relationships with great stretches in between. There the conversation lagged, since aside from Debbie I have no experience of serious, long-term relationships, though I know a great deal about the long dark stretches between.

Around dusk we fortified ourselves with ice cream and started doing our laps. Some of the others joined us for a little while, but mostly it was me and Willy. My friend the Wildebeest is actually very easy to talk to. It made the time a non-issue. He found out all about Doug and Debbie. I found out that his dad died in a freak factory accident when Willy was ten; he was working in a boiler room without harness and the scaffolding collapsed. Makes you wonder how he and his mom have managed to remain so *nice*. Where I come from, a dad's death and a mother's cancer gives you license to be (a) a total asshole and (b) in ongoing therapy.

Sometime before dark the race administrators came around and set up little white paper bags all along the inside of the track. I didn't pay attention until they came round again and lit the tea lights that had been placed inside. I thought at first this was just illumination for the walkers, but you could see the writing on the bags. "To Jeri, we miss you, Bug and Louie and Kip." "For Mom, always with us." Quotes from Garth Brooks songs, a couple from the Dalai Lama. I had to stop reading them. Too many people, too much pain written there for all to see. It's enough to make anybody cry.

I said to Willy, "How do you survive losing someone you loved that much?"

He took my hand. I thought that was sweet.

The night grew quieter and quieter. There were fewer and fewer people. Here and there you could see someone sitting before a camp fire, feet up on a chair, staring into a flame. There were whispers and flashlights moving inside the tents. The stars came out. I wish I could remember everything Willy and I talked about, but then again, those kinds of conversations always sound so stupid in the light of day. There's a shyness that gets to reveal itself inside of darkness. And it doesn't even matter what is said, only that the sounds drift back and forth, and you know that you are speaking into the great wide universe and someone is listening to you.

Around 2:00 am Willy started flagging. He's not an all-nighter sort of person; he's more of an early-to-bed and early-to-rise sort of person, however that happens. We stopped by the campsite for coffee but not even that helped. His mom pointed to the chaise and told him to sleep for an hour and she started walking with me. I thought she should be sleeping, but she said she liked doing these things. She said she'd developed insomnia a few years after her husband died, and she'd started talking long walks at night. She said it made her feel peaceful.

I asked her about her treatments and she told me. I asked her about being married. She told me all about Willy as a kid. He was a science nerd and a soccer player. When his girlfriend broke up with him right before senior prom, he asked his mom to be his date, and she went. They had a great time and she won a TV at the after-prom party.

Around 3:00 I couldn't keep my eyes open, so I woke up Willy and told him to walk the track. This was not an easy task; you know about Willy's sleeping habits. He grumbled, but he got to his feet and staggered away. The rules say someone from the team has to be on the track at all times, or we don't earn our pledges. Willy's dark hair stood out all over in these crazy curls and he had this little-boy grumpy look to him. It was cute. I burrowed into the blanket that he'd left on the chair and not even the four kinds of snoring coming from the tent could keep me awake. The blanket had a warm Willy-smell to it and I didn't fall asleep so much as pass out.

The next bit is the part that is really none of your business, but Harvey reminds me that it is in the interests of literature to tell the truth. There's nothing bare-all about it, fortunately; there were plenty of covers all around. And I might have imagined everything. I mean, I can be pretty groggy when I've had 1½ hours of sleep.

And it's not like anything *happened*. I woke up and I was not alone on the lawn chair any longer. Willy was under the blanket with me, and he was completely zonked out. If you can't see how a 6'4" man and a not-so-wee woman can fit on a little bitty chaise longue, you have to imagine that there is a fair amount of limb twining. It was dark and there was so much quiet, except for Willy breathing straight onto my neck, which made everything seem a lot weirder and, perhaps, more important than it was. I couldn't quite distinguish what was blanket and what was Willy and which limbs were mine as I tried gingerly to untangle.

Somehow I had been lying half on him, but he had one leg flopped over mine, and both arms wrapped around me, probably to keep him from falling off the damn chair. I tried to lever onto my knees and Willy stirred. He's still sleeping, remember. Doug used to grope me all the time in his sleep. It must be some instinctive male response to nearby female flesh. So Willy's hands move down my back and over my rear and pull me tight, very tight, up against him, and that little part of the men that we always make fun of, that has a mind of its own, was giving me the very clear message that not all of Willy was entirely oblivious to the world.

I think I made some expression of dismay; there was some sound coming out of my mouth. I tried to squirm away and he tried to pull me closer. The leg started to roll, then the hips. He pressed his mouth against my neck and in another minute he would have been on top of me and that awake part of Willy would have been right where he wanted to be. In a blind panic I started pushing at his shoulders and yelling, "Who's on the track? Who's on the track?"

I was trying to push him off the chair, but I ended up pushing myself off, and landed with a bump. I leapt to my feet faster than I have ever moved when woken from a dead sleep, and I threw the blanket over his face. Willy just exhaled, rolled over, and continued with his REM cycle. The air was cold and my butt was wet where I'd fallen on the ground and our campfire was out and everyone in the tent was still snoring. Everything was a gritty grey, a pre-dawn cigarette haze. My mouth was dry. I thought that was a myth made up for erotica stories.

Willy's mom was on the track. She smiled at me when I joined her, shivering in my REI fleece. She'd been walking all this time, looking at the lights. I told her she should get some rest and she said the exercise was good for her. We walked in silence. After a while I noticed we were walking in rhythm, matching stride for stride.

She did get tired and I think for half an hour, or an hour, I walked the track alone. Just me. I thought it might be a good opportunity to get my thoughts in order, but there was just a lot of general noise. I hate to say it, but something *had* happened. That is the most pure and powerful rush of sexual arousal I have ever felt in my life. It made my head fuzzy and stayed in my blood for hours, like an echo lingering in the air. Yeah, laugh, girls. I deserve it. Tough lesbian chick Lulu, bowled over by a boy. By Willy.

Here's the funny thing. He didn't realize he had attempted assault in his sleep. The dawn shift took over around 6:00 and somebody made us omelets. Willy yawned and took down the tent and packed up the stuff and walked the final laps with his mom and her best friend, who had been treated for lymphoma years ago. I sat on the chair in the blanket, finishing my omelet. Willy should have been gross, sweaty or grimy or smelly, something offensive. His shorts and T-shirt were wrinkled and he had a shade of dark stubble over his chin, but it made him more appealing, not less. And he still smelled good. Damn him.

I didn't talk to him in the car. He didn't seem to realize I was angry. At the doorway to his apartment he gave me a general, "Thanks for doing this."

"I was on the track more than you," I said.

"My mom likes you," he said, and waved, and shut the door.

I went to my place. I watered Sprout. I showered and put on my favorite cotton pajamas and crawled into bed. Every part of my body hurt and the physical arousal was so strong that I couldn't sleep a wink.

Now what do I do?

August 1

Things are weird with the Wildebeest. He knocked on my door tonight and made me get dressed so we could go to dinner. We went to the steak joint and watched racing and I realized Willy has developed this habit of eating off my plate. I never share food with anyone except Stacey. I think the most horribly intimate and outrageous thing one human being can do to another is reach over and steal one of their fries. He might as well have put his hand down my pants.

You know I also don't typically mind or feel condescended to when men open doors for me—I deserve, after all, to be treated like a celebrity, as do we all—but Willy puts his hand on my back like he's guiding me through. I was so on edge the entire night that I thought I was going to scream.

Then he wanted me to come over and watch the racing highlights and I sniped at him, "We are not an old married couple, you know!" I called Suze. She was no help. When I tried to explain to her how annoying Willy has become, she said it sounded like sexual frustration. Sexual frustration is Suze's diagnosis for everything, as we well know. She could have at least offered her own sweet self as a remedy, as a gesture of our years and years of friendship. Instead, she seems to think I should jump Willy.

That is not the solution to my problem. I don't think.

August 3

Guess what, girls:

Elena is still calling me. The tenor of her messages has changed; it sounds like she no longer wants to talk about the relationship with the basketball girl and now wants to talk about us. What *us*? Where was *us* when Miss Point Guard had her hand up Elena's skirt? I have strong feelings in favor of threesomes and I do think open relationships can work with certain boundaries in place, but I have strong feelings against being the hypotenuse of a love triangle, thank you very much.

I sat down and thought long and hard how I feel about Elena and I'm a wee bit embarrassed to say that I think the best thing I got out that relationship was the polka-dot water bra she got me for my birthday, the purple fuzzy slippers she gave me for our three-month anniversary, and her copy of *Imagine Me And You* which I kept. I have a better and more honest friendship with a straight man I've known a few weeks than I have, or ever had, with the woman who was my lover for nearly three months. That seems both sad and wrong.

Question of the day: Do you think Mary Anne and Ginger ever had an affair while they were stuck on that awful island? They were far and away so much more attractive than any of those bumbling men, it'd be astonishing if they hadn't turned to each other for a little titillation. I mean, come on! Gilligan? Ew.

Thoughtfully,

Lu

August 6

More of the same. Willy treats me like a girlfriend. He seems not to be aware that we are not dating. I wish he would not eat out of my popcorn bowl at the movies. I wish he would stop slinging his arm over my shoulder when we're standing together, like waiting in line to get tickets, and also stop touching his hand to my hip. I wish I could stop feeling so snippy all the time, because I am not a snippy person, but I am so not comfortable with this contact. I am neither a touchy person nor a feely person, as you, dear reader, already know.

August 7

Talked to Rox and Stacey today. Rox is so totally dotty about this pregnancy. She's bragging about her cramps. She actually can't wait to have morning sickness.

She says, and Stacey confirms, that Rox has never been so sex-crazed in her whole life. The other day Rox started trying on some of the Pea Pod maternity wear she got at the Implantation party, but the cute lipstick-pink tee with the built-in bra apparently sent Stacey over the edge and they ended up spending the whole afternoon not wearing any clothes at all.

Disgusting. Happily committed and pregnant people should not feel obliged to dish on the details of their sex life, thank you very much, especially to those of us dying of enforced celibacy.

Razzled, dazzled, and frazzled,

Lu-oh-oh-lu

August 8

Everybody is going insane. Suze invited me over for cocktails and the whole time she just said ridiculous things like, you should tell Willy how you feel about him. Tell him *what?* That he is annoying the hell out of me? She said if I talk about him every minute then I must think about him every minute and I should just get it off my chest. I don't know what she thinks is *on* my chest. Suze has not been herself lately, a little secretive, a little distracted.

Her advice: "Maybe you should just sleep with him and get it out of your system."

HA! Does she know about the viral strain where, if you sleep with him, it just makes things worse?

Then Willy's mom called and invited me to come over for dinner next weekend, and I told her I had to check in with my book editor about our deadline. If I can't continue to be friends with Willy, I don't think I should go falling in love with Willy's mom.

Speaking of moms, mine is turning into a complete beast, a real *vagina dentate*. I think the hot flashes are starting to fry her brain. She's begun ragging on me about when I'm going to settle down, get married, and have kids. I wonder if I need to hire a plane to air the message "LULU'S MOM YOUR DAUGHTER IS A LESBIAN" all over town. Then again, the shock would probably send her into cardiac arrest and I could get charged with secondary manslaughter or some such. Maybe I should have gotten her a vibrator for her birthday. If anyone needs to work off some sexual frustration, it's that dear mother-o-mine.

August 9

Big fight with Willy. HUGE. Wildebeest Willy vs. Lulu the Lioness, a grand-style, knock-down, drag-out fight. In a bar, no less. How classy. Our favorite corner bar, so now one of us can never go there again. It better be

Willy. I refuse to back down.

It was all provoked by the male ego, of course. Ladies, aren't all of our problems provoked by the male ego? The monstrous, looming, ever-growing-and-blocking-out-the-sun, enormous, preposterous male ego?

The conversation went something like this. We were throwing darts at the bar and eating nachos. Willy accused me of eating all the nachos. I was forced to point out that, actually, he had eaten all of the nachos. He had the audacity to order an Amber Bock for me, because I often drink Amber Bock, although I very easily could have wanted something else to drink that night. I blew up when he did the hip thing one more time.

"Why do you keep *touching* me like that?" I demanded.

And here, ladies and gents, is a moment of awful silence, a moment in which it appeared from his expression that someone was pinching the back of the Wildebeest's neck. Hard. I had a fearful thought: William *likes* me. It went like a cartoon bowling ball down my throat and through my stomach. He looked like I held a knife and was about to carve out his still-beating heart and throw it right there on the bar table among the scattered crumbs of tortilla chip.

Then he shook his head and tried to smile and said, "Well, you know, I've never slept with a lesbian. I'm just curious what it's like."

I was eventually asked to leave the bar, but I hadn't actually broken any glasses; I think I just threw the nacho bowl at his head. He's lucky I wasn't holding a dart.

August 10

You'll never guess who I had lunch with today. Willy's mom.

She came to find me at the office, of all things. I thought at first she had come to tell me she never got my pledges for the Relay, though I swear I gave her the envelope. But no, she came to enlist my help in planning Willy's birthday, coming up in September. Are my party planning skills so renowned that people come from far and wide to consult me?

But, during the course of the conversation, somewhere between the mixed green salad (with a lovely honey-vinaigrette dressing) and the creamy fettucine alfredo with white wine and baby clams, two things became clear to me. One is that Willy hasn't always lived here, and in fact moved back from his job in Silicon Valley to be near his sister and her family and also to be near his mom once he learned she needed to start treatment again.

The other is that I am apparently the closest friend Willy has in this whole town, and not only does he talk about me so incessantly to his mother that she thinks he's completely in love with me, but also she is under the erroneous assumption that I am equally in love with him. I hardly felt it my place to correct her, especially since she insisted on paying for the meal, including the wine spritzer I'd ordered as a cocktail and the sorbet I'd eaten for dessert.

So, rather than sticking to my favorite slogan and telling it like it is, I sat there and squirmed for a good hour and fifteen minutes. I hadn't the heart to tell her that Willy and I had a huge fight and I would probably never speak to him again. Instead, there sat your little Lulu, deceptively planning a surprise birthday party for a man I vowed never to see again with a woman whose cancer remission has ended and is looking forward to several months of intense radiation and chemotherapy, if not worse.

It was not one of my finer moments, I tell you. It's too bad she can't adopt me now because Willy let his inner dork out. I want her to put me in her pocket and carry me home and keep me nice and warm for always. Just my luck that I would get involved with a Virgo, the most logical and difficult and hard-to-please of all the astrological signs.

In need of either a deep massage or a good solid kick to the pants,
Loopy Lu

August 11 10:07 am
Maybe I should have slept with Willy before deciding never to speak to him again. For one thing, I would not be in this state of extreme aggravation. For another, my fantastic self would have ruined him permanently for any other girl. That'd show him.

Then again, the sex probably would have been really lousy. Just because he has great hands and great abs does not mean he has a gorgeous everything else.

August 11 6:54 pm
I can't believe how much I am obsessing over this man. The clamor in my head is enormous. I begged Suze to go out for cocktails with me (they wouldn't let me into the corner bar, can you imagine?) so we went down to the gayborhood and checked out our favorite girl bar. But she didn't look at a single girl there, and I didn't think any of them were attractive. What is

with all the lipstick lesbians these days, all these infantilizing outfits and girly pinks and high heels? Where are the good old sneaker-wearing dykes with the square shoulders and the deep voices? Suze was no help at all. She said ridiculous things like, "You just don't know how to have what you want."

I said, "Don't talk to me about the heart and its yearnings. I write the column."

She said, "Well, you're always picking people who don't want you. Now you've finally found someone who does."

I had to escort her back to her apartment; clearly, there would be no further useful conversation with a drunk girl who was not making any sense.

August 11   8:59 pm

I don't want Willy. I mean, I wanted Doug and looked what happened there. I wanted that girl in Costa Rica, and . . . ouch.

And besides, Suze was wrong. Willy doesn't actually want me. Who knows what Willy wants, I mean really. He called four times after our fight and then three times this morning but now I have not heard from him for twelve hours. He's given up. Who wants a man who gives up that easily?

August 12   4:47 am

Howl with me girls, my darlings. Howl at the moon, your deepest, throatiest, despairing, soul-torn howlings. *Hoooooowwww!* Howl, howl, howl.

It happened, the most awful thing, the thing we never talked about because it would be the most awful thing that could happen. It happened. Around ten o'clock last night Rox started bleeding.

Stacey called me because she was throwing up and was too sick to drive so we rushed Rox to the hospital and they did some tests and gave her an IV and some drugs to slow the bleeding and she's sleeping right now because they also gave her something for the pain after we convinced them she was not and in no way would become an opioid addict. Around midnight we had a slight altercation with the nurse who said that visiting hours were over and Stacey said we were family, I was Rox's cousin and she was Rox's wife and the nurse said they weren't really married because they are two women, and Stacey said I will give you a copy of the marriage certificate signed by the Iowa judge and the nurse got all snippy and gave us that *look* and then she brought in a patient liaison who tried to tell us some bullshit that because it was a hospital run by a religious institution they did not have to honor what they considered an immoral law and Stacey started crying and I started my tirade about equality and human rights and loving kindness toward all, and I was so mad I wanted to kick at the walls or throw hand sanitizer.

Finally they called in the doctor and he looked at the both of us, me boiling mad and Stacey with mascara streaked down her face and her ponytail coming down and holding Rox's hand like you would have to cut off her own arm to make her let go, and finally he said to the nurse that he wanted to keep Stacey there for observation because he was afraid she might become dehydrated and if they separated them it might upset his patient. This distracted the nurse with some different bullshit about did she have to admit Stacey then, blah blah blah, but the important thing was that Stacey got to stay.

We've been through all this before, dear reader, and when I've marshaled some of my resources I will say it all again, loudly and with great emphasis, that some people's religious-based definition of morality should not trump constitutional rights and equal treatment under the law, should not trump LOVE, but right now I'm just so discouraged about the heartbreaking unfairness of everything.

We don't know yet what's happening. It's possible the bleeding will stop. It's possible this won't hurt the baby. Stacey's been throwing up nonstop, but I guess the doctor's right, he can pop an IV in her if she gets dehydrated. Aunt Gemma is catching a flight up later, so I told her I'd pick her up from the airport. It's also discouraging to realize you could have been born to your aunt instead of your mother if not for the mischief of Mother Nature.

I know that there are really awful things going on in the world, darlings, some of them happening to you right now, but if you can send a ray of hope and a prayer Rox and Stacey's way, they could really use it. They so much want this baby.

Keeping her fingers crossed,

Lu

August 12 6:06 am

I have to move. I live in a town where a girl can't even find an open convenience store at 5:00 in the morning to buy herself a box of Kleenex. Suze and Vera both have their phones off. There's no way I want to talk to Willy. This is the dark night of the soul, ladies. We are utterly, each of us, entirely cast into solitude, afraid and alone.

August 12 11:42 am

Ah, weariness.

The tests came back. The night doctor says it's a miscarriage, the day doctor thinks it's Rox's period, but the tests agree: there is no baby.

My aunt Gemma made it up all right. I took her bags to Rox and Stacey's house, then took her to the hospital. She's a certified nurse, so they're going to release Rox early and let her go home. I'm not so sure they shouldn't put Stacey on an IV, though.

No baby.

Harvey's been great, at least. He told me I didn't have to come into work for the meeting today. Good thing, since I'm so tired I can barely see straight. He's probably emptying out my candy jar while I'm not there, the little sneak. Ah, well, let him. If he lets me stay home tomorrow, too, I'll take back, in print, every mean thing I ever said about him.

Rox wants to go straight back to the clinic and get implanted the second she can, but Stacey is pretty shaken up by all this. She doesn't know if she'll be ready to try again any time soon, and besides, it's so very expensive, and not a bit of it covered by insurance, maybe not even this hospital stay. I can be there, I can sit in that hospital room, but I really have no idea what they're going through. And it just split my heart open to hear Rox calling all their friends and telling them over and over, "No baby. No baby. There's no baby."

Damn it. I want my mother. Too bad she's such a bitch and would only call it God's judgment or something.

It's the middle of the day and my apartment is so dark and silent. It's like the eleventh circle of hell. There is only me and there is only Sprout, the two of us against the big, faceless, uncaring world.

August 13

So, Willy and I have reached an understanding.

He came to my door last night and when I opened it, he kissed me. He didn't even say anything, he just put both his hands on the side of my face and leaned down and kissed me. I could hear the lights buzzing in the hallway and his hands reached from my chin to my temples and he tasted like cherry soda and you should have heard how fast his heart was beating.

I couldn't believe he would kiss a girl who'd been crying so hard every capillary in her eyes had burst and she'd been unable to eat for twenty-three hours. I couldn't believe how much I wanted him to curl up in bed and just hold me. And he did. It's a lot to ask, but he did. And he didn't say one stupid or banal thing the entire time.

Either Willy talked to his mom, or he reads this column. How else could he have known that I needed him?

August 14

No, my pets, Willy and I are not sleeping together. He's back in the friend zone, that's what I meant by an understanding. He's been so sweet about Rox and Stacey, and that has completely redeemed him in my eyes. But recognizing somebody's sweetness doesn't make you automatically sexually attracted to them. Of course, he seems to have misunderstood that first kiss and now is trying to kiss me all the time, so clearly I have to have a talk with him. He is a lovely kisser, and it's nice to be kissed, indeed it is, but I don't think my career as a lesbian will get very far if I keep making out with Willy at every opportunity. Flutter in the tummy or no.

August 15

Listen up, dears and darlings.

Willy and I are *not* sleeping together. Can we use this forum to talk about something other than my sex life? I mean, I realize that my talking about my sex life has always been an integral part of Lulu's Advice and Chat, but really, aren't you all having exciting sex lives that you want to tell us about? Any good coming out stories? Anyone had a touching vow renewal ceremony they want to tell us about? Any new books, organized rallies, marches or petitions that we should know about? Come on, girls. Don't drive me into Willy's arms with all this hate-speak about betraying the lesbian community.

I know, let's start a Lulu poll. *Girlfriends* liked my bit on sex toys so much that they want me to do a piece on self-pleasure, or flying solo, something Lulu knows a great deal about. But I can't do this on my own, dolls. Help your Lulu out and post a tidbit to our forum, will ya? Favorite toy, favorite technique, favorite lift-off fantasy. Give me something, girls.

August 17

Okay. So. Willy and I had sex last night.

Well, actually, all through yesterday evening, several times in the night, and then today—my God, it's a wonder I can walk. I blame Suze and her advice.

It began as a regular evening, Willy in jeans, me in my favorite yoga pants and one of those wonderful seamless padded V-neck bras that make me feel I own the world and can do anything I want with it. We queued up some Amy Schumer after I won the thumb wrestle. We made sushi and I mixed cosmopolitans and we both took our customary cushions on The Magic Couch and about halfway through one of her skits, near tears with laughter, I looked over at Willy and saw the most intense look I have ever seen on anyone's face. He was watching me watch the TV. I have never been looked at that closely, that thoroughly, that entirely. Everything he was feeling was clear on his face and it was sweet and appealing and the most incredibly erotic thing anyone has ever done to me.

So I kissed him.

And didn't stop.

But—well. I hope I have now managed to get this unaccountable flare of sexual attraction out of my system. It won't happen again. It was just a fluke that it happened in the first place.

Except that I think Willy might have said something to his mom. He told her about Rox and Stacey and she wanted to make them a cake, so this morning he drove me over to her place for brunch and we picked up the cake and took it to Rox and Stacey's and had fruity cocktails. Rox just had fruit juice, she feels much better now, is back on her feet, but as soon as she can sweet-talk Stacey into it she wants to try having a baby again. And it was just so wonderful to see them recovered and like themselves again and happy that I had an extra cocktail or two, and I think they might have guessed something had happened because of the look Willy cannot seem to wipe off his face. And then when he drove us home he came to my apartment instead of his and I hope he knows I don't intend to let him move in or anything, but as a matter of fact he is doing this thing right now where he is kissing my neck and . . .

Wow. Willy's mom must have put something that cake.

But really, it's out of our systems now. Everything will go back to normal. Because I, as we all know, have obligations. I have a column to write. And honestly I don't know what else to do with this boy.

Yours, still and always,

Lu

August 22

All RIGHT already! Jesus, Tex! I have not betrayed anyone. I have not let down the entire girl-loving population. I am and have always tried to be your flag girl, your advocate, your banner waver, your ally, but I am not the spokesperson for lesbians everywhere, and I am not the light of your poor feeble existence. If I am, GET A LIFE.

Yes, Willy is great in the sack. Someone along the line taught him *very* well. I feel like I should write his former girlfriends and thank them.

And no, you do not get the details. I *have* a life.

It won't last. Nothing lasts. That is the one thing we learn as mortals, our blessing and our curse: nothing we have is ours, but nothing. Yes, Willy slept over again last night, but I only had sex with him because he cooked me a fantastic dinner, seared ahi with wasabi sauce and wilted greens and toasted almonds, heavenly. I felt I should do something nice for him in return.

August 24

Hell-O,

All right, just because I have spent the week shagging Willy does not mean we are a couple, nor does it mean we are anything, ladies and germs. Don't we here behind the lavender curtain know better than to go about sticking labels on everything? Good gracious me, you'd with as much hostility as there already is directed at us LGBTQIA+ folk, we would be a little more forgiving of our own. What, do you want me to rename my column now? Bi-bi Lulu perhaps? I'm not a turncoat, I am an example to you all. I am following my bliss, just as my fortune cookie says I should, and just as you ought to as well. Personally, I think that if a few more of you out there were following *your* bliss, you wouldn't be quite so snarky about *mine*. Guess I'd better get that self-pleasure feature out and fast.

August 25

Willy's mom came to the office to take me out to lunch again today. This time we went to the Mexican place and she stuffed me full of burritos and guacamole. Now she wants a theme for Willy's birthday, though I am at a loss to know what a man Willy's age would find acceptable as a birthday party motif. Tiki lights and hula hoops, perhaps? I might be able to dig up a grass skirt and a set of coconuts from some long-past and mercifully forgotten Halloween from my younger and wilder days.

This lunch registered no lower on the Squirm-o-Meter, however. She's talking like Willy and I are committed couple, like we're in love, like we have a future together, oh dear, dear me. How, I ask you, can you tell a woman you really don't expect to carry on a long-term relationship with her son when she's just bought you a pitcher of sangria?

Good thing I'm having great sex these days or I'd be much more frustrated,

Lu

August 28

M'aidez!

Suze isn't talking to me. Vera isn't talking to me. I've tried to have a conversation with them both about how I should call a halt to things with Willy, and neither of them will speak to me. Fine friends I have. Suze opened her door a crack and looked at me and when I started talking interrupted me to say, "Do you or do you not want to be with him?" and I said, "I do, but" and then she said, "There is no but," and closed the door in my face. She didn't even wait to hear me finish: but I'm a lesbian.

And Vera just sighs about Willy's long eyelashes and great butt (and why is she looking at his butt which is no longer hers for the taking, I'd like to know?) and says we are going to have beautiful babies. As if I'd ever entertain such an insane notion. As if I'd ever do anything that would please my mother as much as my getting married and buying a house and popping out a triad of kids just like every other female from my high school class.

September 2

Help.

Today Willy told me he loved me.

Loves me. And it wasn't a post-coital declaration, either. We were having dinner. Actually, we were fixing dinner, at his place, using his Williams Sonoma cookware. I was salting the boiling water for pasta and we were arguing the way we do, as he can be *so* frustrating about the simplest things, and I don't even remember what I said but he slipped one long arm around my waist and kissed the side of my neck—how do they know to choose these vulnerable areas?—and he simply said it, "I love you," like it was the most natural thing in the world.

Which it is *not*, and which I made haste to clarify. You've been with me for two weeks, I reminded him, and he said, yeah, but I figured this out three months ago—again, like it was the most natural thing in the world. I busied myself with chopping the garlic and did some mental calculations and said, three months ago wasn't I yelling at you about setting off the fire alarm? He grinned and said, and you told me I was burning a cheap candle. That won me, right there.

I don't recall what I said at this point—I was a little flustered, my voice rather squeaky—but it was along the lines of, you don't know something like *love* just off the cuff like that, and he said no, not like that, it's nothing formed and nothing you can really put words to, but you just *know*. And I didn't know what else to do—I was standing there holding a chopping knife—so I put the knife down to try to talk some sense into him, and he put his hands on either side of my face the way he does and then kissed me, and by the time we got back to the stove the pasta water had boiled away and there was a fire alarm about to go off again.

I'm starting to think Willy is more grown up than I am. Though I still don't understand how you can just say something to somebody like that? After two weeks?

No wonder his mother is taking me out to dinner everywhere. Her son told her he *loves* me.

I'm going to need a whole lot of chocolate to deal with this.

On her way to the Godiva store,

Looped-out Lu

September 5

Ouch. Ouch ouch ouch ouch ouch.

Rox and Stacey have scheduled another implantation day. Rox got tested and everything looks good and her doctor thinks that what happened the first time is that the egg didn't take and she had a heavier period than normal, but her uterus looks healthy and should be able to support a baby, so hopefully it will burrow in this time.

They both looked so bright as they told me this, sitting on their apricot couch, with afternoon sunlight coming in through the windows and the whole room seeming to smile somehow.

"And," Stacey said, squeezing Rox's hand, "we can always adopt."

I'm so proud of my cousin. They're not afraid of anything, it seems. I don't think they want to have another implantation party, though. I think this time we'll wait till later in the pregnancy to have a baby shower proper.

And then Stacey, the little sneak, took me aside and demanded to know what was going on with Willy. I told her how he's said he loves me and she just nodded and grinned as though she'd expected it all along. I tried to explain to her how it was awful, not good at all but awful, because things can't work with Willy, sooner or later I'm bound to fall in love with a woman and then what will happen to us? And she said, why am I worried about what could or might happen a hundred years in the future, and what do I feel right now?

I couldn't answer that question. I sat there and thought about it, though. And while I was thinking she said, do you love him? And I had to answer honestly. I don't know. These things take a long time with me. How do you ever know anything like that for sure, I mean really? What are the signs? And if you want to be with someone for the long haul, frightful thought, aren't there so many other things to consider—values, background, how you are with money, how often you want to have sex, where do you spend holidays and vacations? Love is love and sex is great, but *being* with someone who at any second could just up and leave you for someone else—the benefits have to be awfully huge to leave yourself open for *that* kind of wholesale devastation.

And that she got all wise and big-sisterly on me and squeezed my hand and said, "Lu. Stop planning for what happens down the road. If you realize at some point that you can't be with him, then you have to be honest about that. But if you enjoy being with him, then just *enjoy* it. It doesn't matter what you call it. If it doesn't hurt anyone, why shouldn't you do the things that make you happy?"

I told her she got that from my column. She laughed and said, "I did."

But but, I said. I could fall in love with someone else. Or he could. I might hurt him. He might hurt me. One of us is bound to screw things up.

Statistically, it's almost inevitable.

Stacey raised both of her perfectly shaped eyebrows at me and said, "You're really going to plan around what *might* happen?"

I almost said, well, yes. Duh. Then I remembered who I was talking to: a woman who had defied our family, her upbringing, the culture, and at that time the law in order to be with the person she loves most in the world and knew was in every way right for her. So I buttoned my lip and shook my head, and I think that was the right answer, because she hugged me and gently pulled on my hair, which is something she used to do when we were kids, and the gesture almost made me cry.

I left her and Rox's place before I realized she was essentially suggesting that if I want to be around Willy, I should just go ahead and be with Willy.

Yikes.

September 7

Funny how things come full circle. The conversation with Willy was easier than I expected. We were making dinner, Indian this time—I was fixing the rice, he had the naan, and I don't know why but it's easy and comfortable to talk about these things when we both have our separate tasks, and he simply looped his arm around me again and said, are you still freaked out because I said I love you? And I said, a little, yes, because it seemed like honesty was called for in this situation.

Then he just gave me this level look kind of like his mom has and said, so are you going to run the next time I say it? I pointed to the hall door and tried honesty again. I'm not sure, I said, but I brought my running shoes. So he went to the door and opened it and threw my new hot pink Nike sneakers into the hallway and then closed the door and said now what? I started laughing and pulled him to me and we didn't even make it to the bedroom that time and I discovered a couple of moves I think the *Cosmo* editors haven't thought of yet, and since the rice was dry and the naan burned to a crisp we went out for dinner at the vegan place, and who should we run into but Elena.

She was with one of her friends from work, and she looked thinner than I remember her being. I certainly wouldn't fit into her panties now. She saw me first, and then she saw Willy, and then she saw the way we were holding hands and giggling and she froze right there on the spot. I always thought this was a figure of speech, dear reader, but Elena went absolutely still.

I would have pulled my hand away if Willy had let go of it. I felt a guilty flush all the way up to my ears. I didn't feel embarrassed about being with Willy. For the very first time in my life, I didn't feel like I had to apologize for wanting the person I wanted. But I hadn't told her I was involved with somebody, so it was a bit of a shock. And if you could have seen the look of complete and utter scorn that came over Elena's face . . .

But I hope you never encounter that, dear reader, not the expression of disdain with which she lashed me, nor the way she turned her back and flounced—flounced, I tell you—out of the restaurant. Willy caught the look on my face and said "what?" and I said "nothing" and he said "no, really what is it?" and I said "an ex" and he said "huh?" and looked at the door, but Elena was already long gone, the air grown still behind the furious swish of her ponytail.

Willy wanted to know the whole story, and I told him I'd tell him later.

That was the first time, dear reader, the very first moment that I personally felt such contempt directed at me because of who I was with. My mother has done a good job of stonewalling me at many points, but Elena's hatred was entire and sincere. We're lucky we don't live in a world where we can be killed because of who we love.

Oh, wait a minute—we do.

September 9

I am pleased to announce that after lengthy discussion, Harvey and I are rebranding "Lulu the Lesbian's Advice and Chat" into "Lulu's Lifestyle Advice and Chat." Same Lulu, but now I get to boss you around about *everything*. My lesbian ladies, I hope you won't leave me, since we've had so many good times together and I'm still me and full of good advice. Harvey and I both want to make this transition as smooth and amicable as possible.

I refuse to apologize to any and all of the men I've bashed on this blog; just because I like Willy in particular doesn't mean I am subscribing to patriarchal control and benevolent sexism and the violence our culture perpetuates daily and silently on women. I resent those who have written in accusing me of being a fraud, of being a political hypocrite, and/or crumpling in the face of overwhelming societal brainwashing and/or pressure. Haven't I said all along that it's about who we love? Lulu is love, people. If you don't believe that, go back to the beginning and read through the archives.

And to show that we're all still friends, reserve your copy of my book *That Girl,* which will be coming out with Glam Girl press this fall. A portion of the proceeds will go to GLSEN to fund their efforts to make our schools safe for all of us who are gay, bi, fluid, trans, questioning, asexual, whatever the little label gets tossed around—we all of us need to stand together on this side of the lavender curtain.

And, for the last time, stop with the wedding bell threats. I am not moving back into mainstream hetero culture. I'm still reeling over the latest issue of *Cosmo* and "How to Set Your Man on Fire." Clearly, I have some catching up to do.

The other thing is, Willy won't let me talk about our sex life online. He is rather old-fashioned and, in fact, oddly chivalrous. I blame his mother for this.

But, ooh! ooh! Guess who I saw slinking out of Suze's room this morning, casting a furtive look down the hallway and clutching her knickers to her capacious chest? Yep—Vera.

Guess I've been wrong about almost everything. How refreshing.

Since we now know I'm bi, maybe Vera can contribute the occasional post on lesbian life, hmmm? In the meantime, look for my new podcast, coming soon, in which I will share advice for navigating our rainbow world. Get that, baby!

Signing off with kisses to all,

Lulu

P.S. Another big event today—Sprout had *babies!* He put out little tendrils and now there are miniature Sprouts dangling in mid-air. It's pretty amazing. I told you Sprout was my soulmate. When I look at him in his little pot I just see a big green spidery bowl of love. If Rox and Stacey and Willy's mom have taught me anything it's this: we have to love as much as we can, with all our odds and ends and strange lumpy parts and lack of a clear pathway. Stacey was right; we can't shield our hearts against disaster. The only way forward is just the next step, heads up, hands open. Our hearts have simply got to grow big enough to hold all this.

ABOUT THE AUTHOR

Misty Urban's short stories have won awards from *New Letters, Indiana Review,* Writers at Work, *The Atlantic Monthly,* and Cornell University, and she was the 2017 recipient of the Great River Writer's Retreat. Her debut collection of short stories won the Serena McDonald Kennedy Award for fiction and was published by Snake Nation Press. She holds a Ph.D. in Old and Middle English Literature from Cornell University and her dissertation, *Monstrous Women in Middle English Romance,* won the D. Simon Evans Award for Medieval Studies and was published by Edwin Mellen Press. A co-edited collection of essays on the medieval fairy Melusine titled *Melusine's Footprint: Tracing the Legacy of a Medieval Myth* came out from Brill in 2017. She is the founding editor of femmeliterate, a website devoted to feminism, literature, and women in/and/of books. When not working on her latest novel, she teaches writing at Muscatine Community College in Muscatine, Iowa, where she lives with a handsome park ranger, two small people who like to be read to, and a rather heavy collection of books.

www.ingramcontent.com/pod-product-compliance
Lightning Source LLC
Chambersburg PA
CBHW060352180626
46817CB00008B/2987